The Invisible Caravan

Janet Pointon

Published by DayStar Books Ltd
PO Box 65275, Mairangi Bay, Auckland 0754

ISBN 9780995111783

Production by Outline Print Consultancy
Printed in New Zealand

Dedicated To My Grandchildren

Rebekah, Charlotte, Finlay, Jasmine,
Joseph, Isabel, Hamish, Bridget

Acknowledgements

I would like to thank Denis Shuker
for encouraging me to write this book.
Also grateful thanks to
George Bryant who spent many hours editing
and processing it.

CONTENTS

1

Sam Hears A Voice

"What"?

Sam woke with a jump, the strange dream still fresh in his mind. The shrill screech of the landline telephone in the hall outside his room rang in his ears. Rolling over he looked at the clock beside his bed and groaned. Three am! His mother's hurried footsteps followed and a moment later the phone was silenced. He strained his ears, listening to her urgent whispering. It must be his father's call from somewhere in the world. Sam sighed and crept out of bed to listen at his door.

"Why won't you tell me where Dad is and why doesn't he come home anymore?" Sam muttered aloud. He gave up trying to listen. It was impossible to hear and he snuggled back under the warm duvet, trying to go back to sleep.

The crazy dream began again. Someone was reaching out towards him. Sam couldn't decide if they were trying to help him or catch him. Then another noise. He jerked awake again. A branch was scraping against his window. Had he heard something else? Was his mother still speaking on the phone? Sam leaned on one elbow and stared into the dark room. He liked all light blotted out for sleeping. Even a sliver of light showing from the hall made him cross.

"Sam." The voice came from… where? It wasn't his mother and there shouldn't be anyone else in the house. He reached out to switch on the light, stretched too far and fell on the floor.

"Oh great!" Sam flicked the switch and light flooded the room. He was alone.

"You are going to meet Jake and Zoe."

Sam felt more curious than frightened. Where did that deep but gentle voice come from? Jake and Zoe? Had he really heard a voice or had he imagined it? There was a feeling of peace in the room. He climbed back into bed and switched off the light to settle back to sleep. Who were Jake and Zoe? He drifted into sleep before he remembered he should have pinched himself to see if he was still dreaming.

"Come on, Sam. Time to get up!" A door slammed. He heard his mother singing loudly in the kitchen.

Sam yawned, stretched slowly, and stood up and dressed. He felt as if he had butterflies in his stomach but couldn't think why. His mother would call this feeling 'anticipation', but what was it for? Then he remembered. Who were Jake and Zoe? He wandered out to the kitchen and saw his mother dressed in her black, work clothes, putting on her coat.

"Power dressing again, Mum?"

"Don't be rude." She paused, "I've left the food on the table for you to make your lunch. I've got to rush. We both overslept."

"Oh yes, the phone call. Dad, I suppose?"

Ignoring the implied question she picked up her bag and gave her son a critical look. "You need a haircut! Try and plaster it down a bit before school. I've got to drop these keys into the Jessop's. The kids are sick and Carol couldn't leave the house to get her new key copied so I've had this cut for them."

She hesitated again, with her hand on the open door. "If I give you some lunch money, you'd have time to drop them off on the way to school. Please?"

"O.K. I'll put this stuff away when I've had my toast."

"Buy something healthy. No pie!" She put five dollars on the table and closed the door behind her. Sam grinned. He'd buy hot chips.

He stood in front of the large bathroom mirror and stared at himself as he carefully combed gel through his thick, black hair. He was tall for his age with dark eyes like his father's.

The strange feeling still hadn't left him by the time he trudged round the last bend in the road and reached the Jessop's. Their drive was narrow and long. Tall trees lined each side and Sam shivered. The day was cloudy and the trees seemed taller and darker than ever. Sam shivered again and pulled his puffer jacket closer. "Spooky," he muttered.

"Wow! Where did that come from?" He stopped in amazement at the sight of a large modern caravan, crammed in the drive between the trees, with no room to spare on either side. Sam ran his fingers over the gleaming white paintwork and squeezed past, trying to look into the darkened glass windows but he could see only his reflected face. He moved on from the vision of the caravan, walked up the stone steps and pressed the doorbell. It boomed loudly inside the house and he stepped back as the door burst open. A short, plump lady with long, blonde hair stood smiling at him.

"Hi Sam. What can I do for you?"

"I'm delivering these keys Mum's had cut for you."

Mrs Jessop stood back and opened the door a little wider. "Oh, that's nice of her. Come in, Sam. The children have been miserable with a high fever but an hour or two ago everything came right. Thank you so much, dear. I'll ring your mother. Would you like to come in and see the twins or are you in a hurry for school?"

Sam shook his head. The twins were three years old. "No, thank you. I need to get going but I do like your new caravan, Mrs Jessop. Are you going away for a holiday?"

"What caravan, dear? We certainly don't own a caravan."

"There's one parked in your drive over there."

Sam turned to point, and then looked confused. The caravan had gone. Just like that. It had disappeared. How could that happen? Was he going crazy and seeing things that weren't there? The butterflies in his stomach were really flying now and he felt scared.

"Show me," Mrs Jessop sounded amazed. She followed Sam down the steps and on to the drive. He felt awkward.

"It's gone. Maybe it was turning around or something. Never mind, sorry. I'm glad you're all better."

He kept walking, feeling as silly as possible. Maybe Mrs Jessop would tell his mother he had lied. Where had the large van gone in the time he had taken to ring the bell? How could it disappear like that? He knew it needed to be towed but he hadn't seen any other vehicle.

It felt like a long walk back to the road and Sam thought a lot about the disappearing caravan as he scanned the rest of the drive and then stared down the road. What had he seen?

He hurried towards the school gate, thinking of the voice last night telling him he would meet some people called Jake and Zoe. All day Sam watched out for any new people but school ended and he still wondered if he had dreamt about them.

"Swimming squad today!" Ben waved, jumped and yelled to Sam. "Did you forget? You've been spaced out all day."

"Oh, yeah. I was thinking about something else." *Jake and Zoe to be exact.* Sam hurried over to Ben. "I had this weird dream last night about meeting someone. I don't know if I was asleep or awake."

"Did they have a name? Was it a girl?" Ben kicked a coke can into the road. A car tooted. "Race you to the pool." He didn't wait for Sam's reply and the two of them pounded down the road with their backpacks bouncing. They swiped their passes and hurried to the changing rooms.

"Well did they?" Ben demanded at the foot of the stairs.

"Did who what?"

"Your dream person. Did they have a name?"

"Two people, called Jake and Zoe."

"Oh well, let's see if we have some new members in the squad today."

For the following two hours Sam had no time to think of anything except his arm and leg movements and his breathing. It was a privilege to be in the squad and there was always someone to take over if he fell behind.

"See you tomorrow, Sam. Your dream people didn't turn up?" Ben pushed past and ran towards his father's car. His head popped back out from the back seat. "Dad wants to know if you want a ride?"

"No thanks, I'm good. Got to look for my dream people!"

They both laughed and Sam carried on towards home.

One street away from his house and outside the

fish and chip shop Sam stopped with a gasp. A large golden labrador lay in the middle of the bus lane. Sam had seen people waiting at the previous stop so he knew there would be a bus due at any minute. There were too many cars for him to cross over.

Then he saw the bus waiting at the traffic lights.

2

Sam Meets Jake and Zoe

"Help! Dog get up so the bus can see you!" This was silly. How could a dog understand human language? Sam's throat hurt with his shouting. Now he saw the bus begin to move towards them. What could he do? He could hardly breathe or believe what he saw next. The dog stood up, wagged its tail and carefully dodging the tooting cars walked calmly over to Sam and sat down, looking at him.

Sam hadn't had much to do with animals but he reached out, hoping this one was friendly, and dragging the dog by the collar he hauled it away from the street.

"Silly dog, keep off the road if you don't want to be squashed."

He kept walking but the dog seemed to think Sam was now his best friend and wouldn't stay away. When Sam stopped the dog stopped and when Sam ran a little way the dog was still beside him. He arrived at his house, still with his companion, and when he opened the door the dog rushed inside first.

It was six o'clock and the noise from his mother's singing was even louder than the CD playing in the lounge. Added to this was the clatter and banging of cupboard doors and saucepans. Only in the middle of the night on the phone was his mother quiet.

She turned and stopped in mid-sentence as the great golden-haired dog brushed against her legs.

"You found Goldie! Where was she? Mrs Harris said she has been ringing everyone she could think of as well as all the shops to see if anyone could find her. Isn't she beautiful?" Essie Burnside buried her face and shoulder length red hair in the dog's coat while Sam looked on with a pained expression.

"What if the dog's got some skin disease like mange or ticks?"

"Oh, Sam. Don't be so miserable! Dinner's almost ready. Get some string from the laundry and tie it to her collar so you can take her home please. Mrs Harris lives opposite the fish and chip shop. Number 80."

"That's where I found her, lying in the bus lane. Then she wouldn't stop following me." He tied the string to the dog's collar and left his bag on the floor. His mother pointed to it and looked at him.

"I'll move it when I get back."

"Now, please!"

Sam grinned, grabbed his bag and ran, dodging her outstretched hand. "OK. You shouldn't still have your work, power clothes on!"

He sang to himself as he walked. There was always music in his house. It would either be his mother singing the latest lyrics, the CD player or the old-fashioned record player turned up full volume. Goldie seemed happy to trot along beside him.

He had almost reached Goldie's house when he heard a slight hum and a pool of light surrounded him. The sunlight was fading and Sam squinted at the brightness.

The caravan had appeared again, near him, with light blazing from the windows, the door, the walls… Sam stared. It was as if the caravan was covered with some luminous substance. There was nobody around and Sam tentatively touched the sides of the van. They were real and felt cold.

He hurried on to Goldie's house, turning around every now and again to stare at the pool of bright light. He knew this must be the same caravan he had seen in the morning and he wanted to watch it disappear but he certainly would not mention it to Mrs Harris. He wouldn't be caught out twice.

The dog seemed to want to stay behind now and Sam had to half drag her to the house. He knocked at the door.

It seemed ages as he waited for several keys to unlock it and for the door to be opened. Sam began to feel impatient. Was the caravan still there? He couldn't tell from the doorstep.

"You've brought her back! Thank you so much, dear." Mrs Harris, who looked about 100 year's old to Sam, beamed with delight.

She reached out to give him a hug but Sam quickly bent down to untie the string on Goldie's collar. He hated being hugged or touched. The dog whined and seemed to want to stay with Sam. Her owner laughed.

"You've made a friend. I'll know who to ask if I ever need to go away. Come on, Goldie. Say good-bye." She took the dog by the collar and pulled her inside the house as she closed the door.

Sam turned to walk back home. Would he still be able to see the caravan? He could! A tall man with dark hair, wearing blue jeans and a white tee-shirt stood beside it and a boy about Sam's age and a slightly younger girl were sitting on the steps.

The man stepped forward.

"Hi Sam. My name is Jon and these are my children…"

"I know. They must be Jake and Zoe." Sam grinned at the man. "Someone told me I was going to meet them. I've been looking for them all day. What's going on? Where do you come from? Whose voice did I hear when I thought it might have been a dream?"

Jon smiled. "So many questions! You must have heard our King speaking to you as we need you to help us. That's what we do. We travel around your world helping people. Not everyone can see us but you can see both other people as well as us. We need to work together."

"We wanted you to see us before the Nix found you."

Zoe jumped up off the step and sounded excited. Jon turned and frowned slightly. He ruffled her short auburn-coloured hair.

"I was going to keep that information to ourselves a bit longer, Zoe, but never mind. Sam needs to know there is an enemy who is working against us all."

"Could Goldie see you?" Sam was intrigued. Who were these people and who were the Nix?

"Yes, animals can see us. We thought we'd say 'hello' today but we'll catch up with you tomorrow. Remember there are only the three of us who you should speak to." Jon and the children turned towards the caravan.

"Wait! How would I know this Nix you talk about?"

The boy, with the curly, brown hair and sparkly eyes, turned to Sam and spoke for the first time. "They look the same as us but usually people can't see them. Animals run away."

The people and caravan vanished – right before Sam's eyes.

3

Sam And The Nix

Next day Sam left the school gate and hurried up the steep hill towards his house. He hadn't seen his new friends in the morning and now he kept checking the road ahead, looking for the caravan.

It might appear anywhere at any time. He waited at the traffic lights alongside a boy on a bike. The lights changed and Sam began to cross.

"Hey, you dropped a book."

Sam turned to the boy and immediately tripped and fell on to the road. The boy reached out his hand and helped Sam up, then dismounted and walked beside him. Together they walked quickly to the other side.

"Sorry, it was only a piece of paper blowing in the wind. Not your book after all. By the way, I'm Nicholas."

Sam was too busy examining his cut knee to speak as even though he had fallen only a moment ago the skin around the graze was bright red and swelling up. Eventually he stood up and took notice of the tall friendly person beside him.

"I'm Sam Burnside. I haven't seen you before. Are you new around here?"

"I saw you at the swimming squad yesterday and I'm having a trial next week. My parents are trying to enrol me at the Intermediate down the road. I've got to have some sort of test as we're not in the right catchment area but they reckon it's a good school. What do you think of it? Are the guys cool?"

"Yep, it's all right. I'll introduce you to some of my friends if you get in. I live near here so I'll see you. Good luck for the squad!"

Sam hurried away. The boy waved, threw his leg over his bike and sped down the road.

Sam's knee hurt, and his head was beginning to throb badly. He also felt a bit sick. The 'friends' he could introduce Nicholas to would be people in his class. Sam didn't have any close friends. He limped towards his house. Jake and Zoe stood in his way. Where had they arrived from? Sam hadn't seen the caravan?

"You spoke to one of the Nix," Jake told Sam. We warned you not to."

"How would I know? He didn't have 'Nix' printed

on his forehead. I feel too sick to talk, even though I would like to ask you so many things." Sam felt cross and tired.

Jake grabbed his hand and held it firmly, causing Sam to stand still. The throbbing in his head stopped and the queasiness eased off.

Sam stared at Jake. "You made me feel better. What happened?"

"I told you. We help people. The Nix are here to steal, kill and destroy everything." Jake reached into his pocket and pulled out a small tube. "Put this ointment on your knee."

"He looked exactly like me. How can you say he steals, kills and destroys. Why don't you try being friends. He said he is new to the district."

"Go home, Sam. If we are going to be a team, as our King wants, you need to trust me. This boy is one of the Nix and if you try and be friends with him he will only cause you trouble. He might look like you. Believe me, he's not."

All this time Zoe had been quiet, staring at Sam with wide, blue eyes. Now she spoke. "Don't make friends or even speak to him, Sam. He's not the sort of person you think he is. In fact he's dangerous. You'd better put that ointment on your leg right now or you'll need the hospital tonight. You must have touched him?"

Sam dumped his bag on the ground and squeezed the tube over the graze. "His name is Nicholas and he helped me off the road when I tripped. Shouldn't I have washed this first?"

"No. You have to get rid of the poison. See, it's already healing. The Nix would have made you trip with some sort of trick."

"Yes, he told me I had dropped a book but I hadn't. Why do you call him Nix?"

"The Nix can appear in any form. You met Nicholas but if you meet another Nix he may look like a girl. Your leg will be fine. Can you come with us tomorrow after school?" Jake studied Sam's leg.

Excitement began boiling inside Sam. "Can I see inside your caravan? Where shall I meet you?"

"I'll be on the steps as you come out of school. Remember, no one can see me so don't start having a conversation or they'll think you're nuts!"

Sam picked up his bag and was about to continue speaking but they had gone. He carried on home, wondering and excited about the new adventures he would be having with his strange friends.

Nicholas had seemed more normal than Jake

and Zoe. He was even trying out for the swimming squad and might also be at his school. What was he going to do? He began to feel a bit scared.

Surely he couldn't be suspicious of everyone he met?

4

Inside The Caravan

Next morning Sam opened his eyes. There was that feeling again. Sort of happy and excited and maybe a little bit scared. Something was different. Then he remembered what had happened with Nicholas and didn't know whether to feel scared or happy. His mother's voice sounded loud.

"Breakfast! Come on, Sam. Time to get up!"

He rolled over in bed and studied his knee. There were no scratches or marks at all on it. He lay back down and stared at the ceiling, then round his room. His clothes were scattered where he had dropped them the night before. The table with his model plane looked the same. Sam stretched slowly and examined his knee again. No trace of any damage. He dressed quickly, thinking about his coming adventures.

"You've got music after school today. Remember? If you would rather give it up you can, you know. You don't do any practice and it's quite expensive for the lessons." His mother passed him a plate of porridge.

Sam groaned. "I'd forgotten the day was changed."

"If you want to stop having lessons then tell the teacher today it will be your last lesson. What do you think?"

"I was going to do something else after school but I don't want to stop playing my guitar…"

"Well, I'm sorry but today Mr Brant is expecting you at four o'clock. You can tell him today if you want to stop but you need to be there at four."

How could he meet with Jake and Zoe and have his guitar lesson as well?

School finished at 3.30 p.m. and, as arranged, Jake stood waiting on the steps. People jostled around as they hurried to the waiting buses. Jake fell into step beside him and Sam waved his guitar case.

"I've got a guitar lesson soon."

"You won't be late. Come on, we're parked by the chip shop. Let's run."

"Don't suppose you could carry my guitar!" They both laughed.

They left the school grounds, turned the corner and ran to the end of the road. A long gleaming white caravan sparkled with light. As they reached it the door opened and Jon stood smiling.

"Hi boys. Come on in." He stood aside.

Sam hesitated and briefly hung back. He met Jon's clear brown eyes.

"It's all right, Sam. You are safe with us," he said softly. "Let this be the last time you are ever afraid. Jake can show you round while I check out our next destination."

Sam took a deep breath and almost stepped inside.

"Hey, Sam! Didn't you guys hear me?" Ben stood next to him, puffing and openly admiring the caravan. He turned to Jon. "Wow, can I look inside too?"

"Come on in."

"Can you see it?" Sam stared at Ben and Jon.

"See what?"

"Never mind. I was thinking about something." Sam followed the others inside, puzzling as to how Ben could also see the van. The two boys stood inside the door looking at the equipment and size. On the outside it seemed large for a caravan but the inside appeared to be as big as a house.

"This is huge," Ben said eventually. "It's not like a caravan in here. It's more like a house. Where do all the doors lead to? Do you have bedrooms?"

"I'll show you in a minute. Leave your guitar near the door, Sam, so you don't forget it."

"I wish I could stay. This place is amazing but I'll have to go as I've got a guitar lesson at four o'clock."

"There's no time in our universe. You won't be late. It will be the same time when you leave the van as when you stepped into it."

"What?" Ben stared at Jake.

"Come and find Zoe." Jake led the way towards one of the doors.

"I'll be with the computer." Jon sat down on a swivel chair in front of a huge monitor.

Jake opened the door and both boys gasped. The door led out to a long, sandy beach with seagulls and warm sun. The surrounding hills were covered with amazing coloured flowers and trees. Far away in the distance Zoe splashed around in the water with a small dog and several others were swimming. A beach volleyball game was taking place on the sand, along with loud shouts of laughter.

"What happened?" Ben squealed, clutching on to Sam. "Did you know about this?"

"Not really," Sam admitted as Jake closed the door. They stared around at the hills and the people lying on the sand, and listened to the shriek of the seagulls.

"Where are we, Jake?"

"Hi there." Zoe came running towards them. "Did you get a big surprise?" She laughed at the expression on Ben and Sam's face. "I'm Zoe. You must be Ben?"

"Where are we?" Ben asked again. "How do you know my name?"

"Don't bother asking. There's a lot we don't know about them!" Sam grinned at Ben.

"We live in a parallel world to yours," Jake explained. "There is a huge difference though. In our world nothing bad can happen. We take it in turns to come through the fabric and help your world. There are lots of other people on this beach but I don't suppose you can see them?"

"I can," Sam answered.

Ben drew a deep breath. "No, I can't see anybody else. What do you mean there is nothing bad? Could you drown in the sea?"

Zoe and Jake laughed happily. "No! Nobody dies here, or gets hurt or sick. That's why we come through to your world to help."

"What happens if you were walking across a road and a car hit you?" asked Sam. "You do have cars, don't you?"

"Yes, we have cars. But we have a sort of force field around us. The car couldn't touch us."

"What if a rock fell off a cliff on to you?" Ben queried.

"It would be deflected," Jake answered. "Do you want a swim?"

"No, we haven't got any other clothes," answered Sam. "Anyway, what about us? We could drown!"

"No. Not in our world," Zoe told him.

"Do you go to school?" Ben wondered.

"Yes, it's all the same as yours but everything is perfect. Nobody in our world has wrecked it as they did in yours."

"What?" Sam and Ben said together.

"What do you mean wrecked it?" demanded Ben.

Zoe and Jake looked at each other.

"They don't even know this," Jake said to his sister, wonderingly.

"Tell us, tell us," Sam said loudly. "Who wrecked our world?"

"Let's have fun," Zoe said. "Forget the past you can't change. Come on. Race you to that seagull."

Ben and Sam stood and watched Zoe run off.

Then they sat down on the warm sand and Jake sat down too.

"I'm having trouble figuring out all the things you've been telling us," Sam said thoughtfully. "Can we go back in the caravan and talk? I'm sort of hoping I can get back home."

"Are you coming?" Zoe ran back to them.

"Not at this minute, Zoe. We're going to show these guys our computer and the rest of the caravan. You'd better come with us as I think we must have a mission."

"Where's the doorway we came out of?" Ben stared at the beach scenery. "Where's the caravan?"

Jake reached out and turned an invisible handle. A door opened into the caravan and the four children trooped inside.

Jon met them in the doorway. "Come on in, guys, we've got work to do. I was on my way to find you."

5

A Tsunami

Jake closed the door to the beach and Jon led the way to a main lounge. Suddenly they heard a loud humming.

"That's our computer telling us we have an immediate assignment. The computer begins humming and numbers flash across the screen, telling us our location and destination."

"Printing beginning!" shouted Zoe in great excitement.

"What is it printing?" queried Sam. The flashing numbers on the screen meant nothing to him.

"It's our job," explained Jake. "When we get the printout we'll know where we will be going next. It might be anywhere."

"Does that mean we won't see you again?" asked Ben sadly. "I thought we were going to explore your world."

"You can come with us," Jake said happily. "We'll

be in your world but we can pop into ours for some extra fun if you like."

"Our parents won't let us go away with you," Ben declared. "We always have to say where we are, and we need to go back home tonight."

Zoe laughed and clapped her hands. "Oh, you don't understand," she said. "Of course you can come with us. We may be away for several days but it will only be a few minutes in your time. We're going to have lots of fun. Let's see where we go first."

She reached out and took a sheet of paper from the lower part of the computer and handed it to her brother.

"We're going to an island where a tsunami is heading and we need to move fast."

"What's a tsunami?" Ben asked Sam quietly.

"It's a tidal wave," Sam explained. "The sea goes a long way out and a huge wave comes crashing back to the beach."

"Are you guys coming or not?" Jake turned to Ben and Sam who looked at each other and shivered.

"Yes, I suppose so," they replied a little uncertainly. "Where's Jon?"

"He's doing something else first."

Jake reached over and pressed a red switch on the side of the computer. Sam hadn't seen this before and he stared in amazement as a picture appeared on the large screen. A low hum filled the van and for a few minutes they watched in silence as the screen filled with a picture of the sea and clouds and some islands in the distance.

Finally, an island covered in tall, green trees took up the whole picture.

"Is this where we're going?" asked Ben.

Jake turned to him and grinned as the picture showed the ground approaching fast and then they saw a huge flat area on a sloping, tree-lined hill.

"This is where we are. You were watching the screen as we flew to the island." Ben and Sam stared wide-eyed at their new friends.

"Come on, let's open the door and show you." Jake grinned at their surprise, walked over to a door, turned the handle and pulled it open. The scenery they saw was the same as that on the computer screen.

"Whew." Ben and Sam followed Jake outside and stared around. The heat hit them as if they were in front of an oven with the door open.

"You'll need to change your clothes into summer

ones," Zoe called from the door. "Come on, we need to hurry to save these people from the tsunami."

"How can we save them?" asked Ben, returning to the caravan.

Zoe handed him a shirt and shorts.

"There are some sandals in the drawer. You can help us."

"My feet are quite big. These mightn't fit." Sam held the sandals up to see the size.

"They'll fit any size foot, the same as the clothes." Jake stopped halfway through the door.

A few minutes later Ben and Sam followed Jake and Zoe as they hurried down the grassy hill. In front of them and on the other side were a group of sheds. In the distance they saw what appeared to be a small town and in front of the shops and houses at the end of the long hill was the sea.

Hundreds of people, with many mothers holding little children, stood pointing towards it and as Ben and Sam turned to look they realised they couldn't see any water. It looked as if someone had pulled the plug out of the bath.

"Quick, follow me," shouted Jake and he began running down the slope towards the empty bay.

"The water will come rushing back in about five minutes. We have to stop it."

Ben and Sam looked at each other and at their friends running down the hill. Ben suddenly began hurrying after them. He turned back to Sam who hesitated at the top.

"Come on, Sam. They said we would be all right. Let's see what happens."

"But this is our world, not theirs!"

They reached Zoe and Jake who were now standing at the bottom of the hill looking out to sea. A huge wall of water seemed to be forming on the horizon and they were aware of the wind beginning to whip up the sand in front of them.

Ben and Sam gasped in horror at what they saw.

"I don't like this," whispered Sam as he began to back away from the beach.

Ben stared in astonishment as Zoe and Jake reached out their arms and began to speak together, looking towards the water. Their voices sounded like a roar.

"Go back, wall of water. Go back to where you came from. Peace to this land and these people!"

Slowly the sea began to trickle back to the beach

although the huge wave of water now looked even higher.

Both Ben and Sam turned and ran as fast as they could back up the hill towards the people they had passed on the way down. Would they be out of reach when the tidal surge struck the beach? The roar of the water now filled the air and they heard frightened screams from the people above.

"Don't look, don't turn around," Ben had barely enough air left to speak and both boys were now sobbing in terror.

"I can't run anymore and I can't look behind," Sam gasped, flinging himself down on the dry, brown grass. "Where's the caravan? It doesn't seem to be here anymore. Oh no," he groaned. "I haven't told you about the part where it becomes invisible, have I?"

6

Ben Gets Mad

Ben sat down beside him without answering and for a few minutes neither spoke.

"Sam," Ben began eventually. "Sam, look at the sea. The big wave has gone."

Sam spun round and sat up. Ben was sitting, staring straight ahead.

"Ouch!" Ben jumped up as a sharp stick poked his shoulder. A tall bronzed man with bone earrings stood above, signalling to a nearby group of men and boys. Within seconds they were surrounded by dozens of people, all talking loudly in a strange language.

"Quick, run," yelled Sam. Both boys leapt to their feet and charged through the group.

"Where can we go? Where's the caravan and where are Zoe and Jake?" Ben sounded frightened.

"There are some sheds over there, quick," puffed Jake. "These people don't look too friendly."

"There's nowhere to hide," Ben whispered

nervously as they huddled against the back of one of the sheds. "Hope they don't follow us."

"These look deserted. Let's see if we can open the door and go inside to hide under something in there," Sam suggested.

"Wouldn't it be better to make for the trees?"

"No time. They'll see us before we reach cover. Come on, quick."

The two boys rushed to the door and to their surprise and relief it opened easily.

They stood inside the shed, blinking and unable to see for a few seconds after being in the bright sunlight. Sam seized hold of a brightly-coloured mat and pulled it on top of them. They lay on the floor trying desperately to control their breathing. They could hear shouts outside and running feet. Gradually they felt calmer with their pursuers crashing around in the bushes behind the sheds.

"What will we do?" whispered Ben. "How will we find Jake and Zoe?"

"Remember their computer? They should be able to find us," Sam whispered back hopefully. "I'm getting a bit hot under here."

"Hey, stop treading on my fingers," Ben hissed suddenly.

"How can I tread on your fingers?" Sam rolled his eyes. "I'm lying down here..." Suddenly both boys shuddered as they realised they were not alone.

A small girl with long, black hair and eyes full of unshed tears stood staring at Sam and Ben's frightened faces. Ben nodded towards his fingers which were still under the child's chubby bare feet. She stepped back and, putting her thumb in her mouth, continued to gaze at them with wide, brown eyes.

Outside, there were clear sounds of the people calling someone's name but the girl made no effort to move.

"They'll think we kidnapped her," Ben wriggled out from underneath the mat and stood up. "We'd better get out of here as soon as we can."

Sam joined him at the doorway and together they peeped through.

"Nobody there, let's go," whispered Ben. "Head for that clump of trees."

Without a backward glance they charged out of the shed and, puffing and panting, ran as fast as they were able and threw themselves to the ground at the edge of the nearest bushes.

Something soft plumped down beside them. Aghast, Sam turned to see the girl had followed.

"She's here too. What are we going to do? How can we stop her following us?"

"We have to run faster," Ben said. "She's only little. She can't catch up with us if we don't stop."

"But she'll get lost," Sam argued.

"So, what are we going to do? Tie her up?" He glared at the child. She seemed to be like a shadow that was connected to them. Her tears rolled silently down her face as she stood next to them with her little thumb stuck firmly in her mouth.

Sam sighed and reached out for her hand. The girl hesitated and then took a step back.

"Good, we know how to get rid of her. Just try to be friendly." Ben sounded cross. "Come on. Let's go to the next clump of trees."

"We must be getting further and further away from the caravan. How about we stay here?"

"You can if you like." Ben sounded furious. "I should never have come to this stupid place." He leapt to his feet and sped away. Sam sighed and looked at the girl.

"Go home," he told her firmly, pointing back the way they had come. The child showed no sign of understanding and continued to stare at him.

Sam lay on his stomach. He couldn't see Ben and had no idea how far ahead he was.

"Zoe, Jake," he whispered softly. "Come and help us, please. I'm scared to leave this kid here and I'm scared to keep going with her following me. Zoe! Jake!"

Someone grabbed his foot and he swung round. Jake stood grinning at him.

"You've got the idea," he said. "We heard you call. I'm glad you've got Nimra with you." He reached out and took the girl's hand. "The other thing we had to do was take her back to her own family. She was kidnapped as part payment of her father's debt."

"Kidnapped?" Sam glanced at the girl who now clutched Jake's hand. "Are you sure she didn't wander over here? She's been trying to follow us for ages."

"No, they took her. Where's Ben?"

"Don't know. He got so mad he ran off. Can't you find him too?"

"No. He didn't try and call us. You did," Jake pointed out. "Come back to the van and we'll leave Nimra with Zoe for a while."

"Where is it? We couldn't see it."

"You could have if you had tried a bit harder." Jake sounded firm. "When you are scared you stop yourself from being able to do lots of things. It's right behind us now."

Sam stood up and brushed off the dry grass. The gleaming, white caravan in the clearing behind made all his remaining fears evaporate. He wondered if it had been there all along.

"How are we going to find Ben?"

7

A Dangerous Mission

"Come on." Jake took the little girl by the hand and nodded to Sam. "We need to take her to the caravan, and then you and I can search for Ben."

"Can't I stay with Zoe?" Sam moved the bushes apart and glanced anxiously around.

Jake had begun walking away. Now he stopped and faced Sam. "You need to come, as Ben is so angry and mad he won't be able to see either me or the caravan. Do you remember how neither of you could find us as you ran up the hill? Bad feelings of anger or fear block you being able to see us. Has Ben been your friend for very long?"

"No," Sam said sadly. No, I don't know him very well. We swim together."

"Well, come on," Jake said firmly "We need to hurry to save him. Be careful with Ben. I think the Nix may have talked to him."

Sam hurried along beside Jake and the girl. He sighed with relief when they reached the caravan, glad he was able to still see it. Zoe opened the door and gave her brother a hug.

"Hello Sam. Jake, Dad wants us to take this little girl to her family as she has been kidnapped and they are very sad about it."

"Okay," Jake turned to Sam. "We'll find you in a few minutes, Sam. Go back and begin searching for Ben. I'll come to you soon. Remember, keep happy, knowing that I'm coming. Then everything will be all right." He touched Sam's hand as he spoke, and suddenly a surge of joy swept through him. Sam no longer felt hungry, thirsty or tired.

"How come Nimra can see you?"

"Little kids usually can, until they get too much into your world."

"I'll go and find Ben, then. See you soon," Sam said cheerfully. Waving goodbye he ran back the way they had come.

"Ben!" He called as he reached the bushes. "Where are you?" He no longer had any fear of being lost or captured by the tribal people. Further and further into the bushes he rushed, pushing them aside, uncaring as his legs and arms became more and more scratched.

"Ben."

Suddenly he tripped and stumbled headfirst into a large hole. Sam lay in the prickly stony hole for several minutes, letting his breathing recover. He knew he hadn't broken anything although the scratches were beginning to become very uncomfortable.

Eventually, he pulled himself up and hauled himself out. Silence. He listened again.

There were no birds or people anywhere; only scrubby bushes and rocks with large prickly plants.

"Ben!" Sam bellowed at the top of his voice and then stopped to listen. Nothing.

He began to move forward again and pushed aside the nearest bush. Suddenly he stopped. The small bush was on the edge of a very high cliff and if Sam hadn't fallen into the hole he would have gone flying over the side. He didn't know whether to feel terrified or grateful for his uncomfortable tumble.

He sat back down on the stones to think. Where was Ben? Perhaps he hadn't realised how close he was to the edge either?

Behind him Sam heard a scattering of stones and heavy footsteps coming his way.

Two men appeared before Sam had time to find a place to hide. They carried guns and wore green clothes. Sam saw all this at a glance but then his gaze became riveted on the third man with a body of someone slung over his shoulders. It was Ben. The men seemed to be as surprised to see Sam as Sam was to see them. One of them lifted his gun as Sam came towards him.

"That's my friend, Ben. Give him to me." Sam stood up straight and pointed at Ben.

The man grunted and laid Ben on the ground. Sam knelt down and stared at him. Ben's eyes were closed and there was a bruise on his head. He was breathing, but looked very pale.

"Jake, Zoe," Sam shouted as loud as he could and to his amazement the three men turned and fled. Sam saw Ben's eyes flutter and then open. He sat up and clutched his head.

"What happened? Somebody hit me."

"Don't worry. I've called Jake and Zoe, so they won't be long."

"I hate it here, I want to go home," Ben moaned.

"Can you walk?" Sam asked.

"I'm dizzy. Can I lean on you?" Ben pulled himself up and clutched Sam's arm. "Let's get out of here," he growled angrily. "Jake and Zoe shouldn't have left us."

"You took off," Sam reminded him as they stumbled through the bushes.

"I wasn't going to stay behind with that stupid girl." Ben sounded mean and nasty.

"Here we are," Sam sighed with relief. "Here's the caravan."

"Where?" Ben looked around wildly. "I can't see it."

Sam held tightly to Ben. "Keep holding me. We're about to go through the door. Perhaps you'd better close your eyes so you don't get scared."

Sam pulled open the caravan door with one hand and held firmly to Ben with the other. He grabbed Ben tightly, helped him inside and guided him to a seat. Jake and Zoe were standing in front of the huge computer with the little girl between them.

"Won't be long," Jake said over his shoulder. "We're just waiting for Nimra's mother to get home."

"Ben can't see the caravan," Sam told him. "Open your eyes, Ben, and tell me what you see."

"I feel funny and everything is cloudy." Ben sounded scared. "I want to go home."

Jake walked over to Ben and touched the bruise on his head. It vanished immediately.

"We're back now, Sam. You'll still be in time for your four o'clock guitar lesson. Don't forget to take your guitar with you!"

"Will I see you again?"

"Yes, of course we'll see you again soon. Don't worry. We need you!"

Sam opened the caravan door and helped Ben out. "Sit here on the grass for a minute."

"That's better," Ben sounded normal. "I'm all right now. I couldn't see or hear Jake or Zoe or see the caravan. Wasn't that weird? I feel as if I've had a nightmare. I'm going to go home now."

Sam froze all through his guitar lesson, wishing he had remembered to change back into his warm clothes. In spite of running all the way home he shivered as he reached his house and checked the letter box for mail.

Again, no mail from Dad. Sam tried to open the door, then sighed as he realised in his hurry to leave that morning he had forgotten to take his key with him. Now he was locked out and all the windows were closed.

He sat down on the top step to think about his recent experiences with Zoe and Jake. Where would his next adventure take him? It was funny about

Ben, though. What would he say to the others at school?

"Hello, Sam. Did you forget your key?" Sam came out of his daydream to see his mother walking towards him. She suddenly stopped and stared. "Where did you get those clothes? You must be freezing?"

Sam jumped up, still shivering in the summer shorts, shirt and sandals he was wearing.

"I'm an idiot. Here I was sitting here freezing! I'll take these clothes back and see you later, Mum," he called, running to the shed for his bike.

"Here, catch!" his mother threw her key to him. "Be back soon. It's almost dinner time."

Sam waved his arm and carefully checking the road for traffic he rode towards the fish and chip shop, disappointed to find nobody appeared to be about. He dismounted from his bike and closed his eyes so he could concentrate.

"Jake, Zoe?" he murmured quietly.

"Hi!" Sam heard a cheerful voice behind. "We thought you might come back. Bring your bike. We're round the corner." He turned to find Jake standing grinning at him.

"I've got a few minutes before dinner so I thought

I'd come back and see where else we can go!" Sam forgot about being cold and the reason he called them.

"You might want to swap your clothes too?" Jake laughed. Sure enough, as they turned the corner Sam saw the large, white, gleaming caravan. Zoe sat on the steps waiting and then ran towards them.

"Hey, you're back. We've got another mission, Jake. It's just come through. Bring your bike into the van, Sam."

8

The King's Country

"Ben's not very happy about things," Sam began awkwardly.

"No, we knew that was going to happen," Jake said quietly. "In fact in a few days you may have to come with us to rescue him."

"Why me?" Sam sounded surprised. "How do you know this?"

Zoe pointed to the large computer screen. "That's how we know," she said.

"Why me?" Sam asked again. "What's he going to do?"

"We don't tell people what is going to happen in the future," Jake told him. "We know the future which is why we are never scared or worried about what's going to happen. The reason Ben will need you is that he won't be able to see us so we can't help him. Unless, of course he changes how he is," he added.

"Where are we off to now?" Sam stared at the

glowing screen, losing all fear of his unusual companions and their strange vehicle.

"We're going back to our world. We have to collect some stuff for Dad," Jake answered. "In your time it will only be about five minutes so don't worry. Better change your clothes because that's why we may have trouble with Ben. The material is different from yours."

"I'd love to come with you but why don't I ride round to Ben and pick up the clothes and take his own to him?"

"Good idea, but too late," Jake sighed. "Never mind, let's go and have some fun. We'll show you our house and where we go to school."

"Fantastic!" laughed Sam. "Where do we start?"

Zoe reached up and opened the door of the caravan. "Here we are," she squealed, jumping out.

Sam and Jake followed and Sam found they were on a grassy area like a park, with flowers of all colours surrounding them. He could see an ordinary-looking rooftop of a house, with a hedge on all sides.

"Is this where you live? It looks the same as my world."

He felt a little disappointed, although the colours were extraordinary. Sam realised he had been hoping for signs of aliens or at least something different from what he knew.

"What's that lovely smell?" Sam held his head high, sniffing around in the air.

"The flowers!" laughed Jake. "Aren't they great?"

"We have to pick up the new phone for Dad," Zoe reminded her brother. "We'd better do that first."

"You have shops?"

"Come on," urged Zoe, running ahead.

"We'll show you." Jake grinned at his new friend. "Come and see."

Now Sam could see another building nearby, with large picture windows. He followed Zoe and Jake more slowly, staring at his surroundings. The colours of the grass, flowers and sky were incredible. And the smell. His mother would call it fragrance, he thought. And wouldn't she love it here. Were his new friends and their country a secret he wasn't allowed to share?

Now Sam could see the shops, large and small, lining both sides of a road, just an ordinary road like his.

"Come on Sam. We're going into this one." Jake tugged at Sam's arm.

Sam stood still and studied the building beside him. It was long and low, and as he looked harder it appeared to shimmer. He reached out to touch the brickwork and gasped as his hand slid straight through. Maybe things were not quite as simple as he had thought.

"My hand went through the wall!" Sam stared at Jake and Zoe. "It looks solid but my hand went through." He examined his hand and wondered whether they would use a door.

Even as he thought this an opening appeared in the side of the building and the three of them walked inside. It was like a big, light warehouse. Shelves lined both sides, filled with nothing Sam could recognise. Leaving him to follow slowly and stare at all the shelving in the shop Zoe and Jake walked to the end where a man sat at a desk with a computer.

"Hi guys. Have you come to pick up your dad's phone?"

"Yes, please. This is our new friend Sam. We brought him with us in the van. Sam, this is Mitch. Sam!"

"Oh, sorry. Hi Mitch. I was just wondering what was on the shelves. I can't recognise anything."

Mitch reached over and shook Sam's hand. Sam felt a warm buzzy feeling run up his arm and into his head.

"It's not very often our King lets anyone through," he said, holding on to Sam's hand. "You must be a special sort of person. Our technology is more advanced than in your world. That's why you can't tell what anything is."

He let go and turned to Jake. "The phone your dad wants is the one on the second shelf behind you. You can take it now. I've checked it out."

Jake bent down and picked up a small box from the shelf. "O.K, thanks, Mitch. See you later."

"Bye," Mitch answered. "Nice to meet you, Sam."

Sam was quiet as they left the shop, wondering what had happened to him in there. The buzzy feeling had left him but he felt light and wonderful and happier than he had ever felt in his life.

"What happened when Mitch touched me? I feel like so happy. More than happy. Is that possible?"

"There's a difference between being happy and being joyful," Jake explained. "You feel happy when good things happen to you but you can feel joyful even when you're having a tough time. Our King is the one who gives us joy."

"That was Mitch, though."

"Everything comes from our King. You are a special person, Sam, because you can hear our King speak. Most people don't listen to him even when he speaks to them."

"I dunno. Sounds complicated that thing you said about joy and happiness."

Sam stared around the street.

"You didn't pay for the phone? Do you use money? Or what do you use instead? And I don't know anything about your King."

There was too much to look at to stop and get answers. Cars were parked but he couldn't see any meters. As he watched he saw a lady with a small child come out of a shop and go to one of the cars. She stopped as if she was about to open the door and then changed her mind and opened the door of the one behind it.

Sam watched as she drove away, noticing the green light on the top change to red when she pulled out on to the road.

"Why have some cars got red lights and some have green," he asked Jake. "Why did that lady almost use someone else's car," he added.

"Everything here belongs to all of us," Jake replied.

"The cars with red lights are parked briefly while the driver is inside the shop. When we finish with the car we put the green light on and it is available for anyone. And no, we don't use money."

"How do you buy groceries and things?" Sam was beginning to think that perhaps, after all, this place was different.

"We collect them from the store and they are checked out on the computer so we don't ever run out of anything. The computer takes it off the stock, you see," Jake explained.

"Where is your King? Where does he live?"

Zoe and Jake laughed happily. "He is wonderful," Zoe said, her eyes shining. "He's the reason you are here, you know. We never do anything he wouldn't want us to do. When you called Jake to help you find Ben our King answered and sent Jake."

"I don't understand..." Sam began.

Suddenly Jake turned to Zoe. "We have to go," he told her quickly. "Come on, Sam. We'll bring you back here another time if our King lets us. We've got an emergency right now. Run to the caravan."

9

Rescuing Ben

Sam wriggled uncomfortably in his bed. Something sharp seemed to be poking him in his side. He shook it off, rolled over and had almost sunk back into a deep sleep when it happened again. Sam woke suddenly and sat up. Jake stood next to him, standing in a pool of light.

"What's happened? It's the middle of the night!" Sam rubbed his eyes.

Jake sat down on the bed and Sam could see the serious expression on his face.

"Sorry to wake you but we need your help."

"My help! How on earth can I help you?" Sam thought of the caravan, the computer which could take them anywhere in a twinkling of an eye and stared in amazement at his new friend.

Jake laughed quietly. "You said that right. You are from earth so that is why I'm here. You are our link to earth people. You can see and talk to us and also to the people on earth. Ben is in terrible trouble and we need you to help him escape. Can you come with me now?"

Sam scrambled out of bed and grabbed his clothes. "Tell me what's happened while I get dressed," he whispered. "Don't wake Mum up though."

"Ben tried to sell the shirt, shorts and sandals to some people and they are keeping him captive until he leads them to us. Of course he can't do this as even if we stood in front of them they wouldn't be able to see us. He has also been speaking to the Nix."

Sam grabbed his jacket from the cupboard and turned to Jake, thinking of Nicholas. "Do you mean he has spoken to Nicholas? Or someone else?"

"It doesn't matter what their name is. They are a group of beings we call Nix."

"What will they do to me then?" he demanded.

"Are you scared?" Jake asked carefully.

"No, I was wondering how you're going to get both of us out."

"Whew. You had me worried for a moment. The answer to being safe is not to be scared. We can see you and will come to you any time you whisper our name. Our King is always listening and will tell us as soon as you need us. Probably before you actually call for us," he added thoughtfully. "Come on. The van's outside so follow me."

"What's that about your King? And anyway how did you get in?" Sam asked as they quietly closed the outside door.

"I have a special vibrating screw driver which can undo any lock," Jake answered.

"Like Dr Who?"

Jake paused. "Who?"

"Never mind. It's a television programme."

They walked down the path and Sam could see the light from the caravan pouring out, changing the darkness into a well-lit road.

Zoe met them at the door. "Hi, Sam. I'm so glad you came. We should have made Ben leave anything from the caravan behind. He's in danger."

Sam climbed up the steps into the caravan and gasped in amazement. There always seemed to be another surprise in store for him.

"Where does the light come from? The van is all lit up but there aren't any lights!"

Zoe and Jake grinned at his amazement. "We don't need to use electricity. Our light comes from within," Jake replied.

"Oh, that's why you had light all around you when you were in my room. It flows out of you as well?" They nodded.

A beep from the computer made them jump. Jake ran over to it and took a piece of paper from the printer.

"We're off. Ready, Sam?"

"Yep, I'm ready. Tell me what to do when we get there."

"Well, the plan is to let you out at the warehouse where the men are interrogating Ben and for you to take it from there. If you feel threatened, call us. OK?"

Sam felt excitement rise inside. "Are we there yet? Oh, I forgot. What about the Nix?"

Jake opened the outside door. "Our King has dealt with them. They won't be bothering you again."

They were on one of the city wharves, surrounded by cranes and container units. Jake pointed to a dark, quiet street nearby. "You need to go inside the warehouse with the cars parked outside."

"See you later." Sam leapt outside. "I'll go and get Ben."

"And the clothes!" Jake called softly after him.

Once the caravan had left the only light came from a single yellow bulb, high up above the buildings and the whole area became as dark as the nearby street.

Sam could see a large container ship being unloaded by crane across the water at the next wharf. It rumbled and squeaked as the wharfies guided the crane driver.

He made his way to the place Jake had pointed out and then turned to see if he could see the caravan. It had disappeared. Sam walked quickly up to the tall, brick building, squared his shoulders and tried the warehouse door handle. It was stiff and noisy but he managed to open it and then creep inside, hoping nobody heard him.

Instantly he became aware of a lot of shouting. He crept forward and peeped into the nearest room. Three men stood over a terrified Ben. His legs and arms had been tied to a chair and the men, wearing jeans, tee-shirts and hoodies appeared to be furious with him. As Sam watched, one reached over, yanked off one of Ben's shoes and began burning his foot with a lighter.

"Hey," Sam ran forward, shouting. "Stop that. What do you think you're doing?"

The men turned and Ben began yelling, "That's one of them. Ask him!"

"Is that right?" asked one of the men. "Are you an alien?"

"I feel like it," replied Sam. "That boy there is a thief but he is my friend, Ben. I've come to help him and to take back the clothes he took."

The men looked stunned. "We paid this kid for those clothes and we want to know where they came from." The tallest of the three advanced towards Sam.

"Take the money out of his pockets, give me the clothes, untie Ben and I'll tell you what you want to know." Sam stood firm.

He was excited to see how Zoe and Jake would get them out of this, but he wasn't scared.

"You're only a kid. Why should we do what you say?" A younger man, without a hoodie, stood in front of Sam, tattooed snakes on his folded arms.

"If you want me to tell you, give me the clothes. I don't care if Ben keeps the money or not. I suppose you'd better untie Ben too."

The man nodded to the others. "Give him the clothes."

"Don't give them to him. He'll go away and leave

me here and I don't know anything. He's the one you want," yelled Ben.

"There you go," the man said roughly, handing the shirt and shorts to Sam. Now tell us where they came from."

"I need the shoes as well and Ben untied." Sam stood firm.

An older man tossed the shoes to Sam, while another untied Ben. Ben stood up and walked over to Sam, without looking at him.

"Sorry, Sam, I was scared," he mumbled.

"Give them the money," demanded Sam. Now Ben did look at him and glared.

"Why should I?"

Sam hit him with the bundle of clothes. "Just do it," he said.

The three men stared at the boys in amazement as Ben took out a bundle of notes and threw them on the floor.

"What's going on with you two?" one asked.

The man with the tattooed arms grabbed Sam. "Tell us what we want to know."

Sam shook off his arms and looked around the large warehouse. "Come in further and I'll show you." He grabbed Ben by the arm and walked towards the centre of the room. "Jake," he muttered.

The gleaming, bright caravan appeared in front of them and, holding Ben and the clothes firmly, Sam opened the door and stepped in. Ben stumbled as Sam hauled him inside.

"What… I can't see anything. Where are we? Where are the men?" Ben sounded frightened.

Jake and Zoe stood quietly over by the computer. Sam dropped the clothes on the floor and handed Ben his own. Jake waved and signalled him to open the door and lead Ben outside.

Sam noticed they were in his drive. Time-travelling again, he thought happily.

"I'm going back to bed. See you some time, Ben."

"What happened? Where are we?" Ben sounded confused.

"You got rescued, that's what happened. This is my house. You can make your own way home. Bye."

Sam ran down the pathway, hoping he would be able to open the door. It opened easily. He closed it behind him, leaving a bewildered Ben in the drive. Sam's bed was calling him.

10

Fight With Ben

Sam was busy with the swimming competition for the next two weeks and beginning to think he had dreamt the whole adventure with Zoe and Jake except that Ben wouldn't speak or go near him. Even at the pool Ben refused to speak.

One day Sam saw Ben walking along the road ahead of him.

"Hey, wait for me, Ben," he yelled, sprinting towards him. Ben turned and then like a startled hare began running away as fast as he could. Sam ran faster, eventually catching up with him.

"What was that all about?" he gasped. "Why didn't you want to talk to me?"

"I don't want you near me. Go away. You and your silly ideas. You're crazy." Ben pushed Sam away but Sam gripped his arm.

"Let go, you moron," shouted Ben. "I'll tell my dad and he'll come and beat you up."

"Why? What have I done? It was you who stole

the clothes and…" Sam began but Ben had covered his ears.

"I don't have to listen to you. Go away. Those people weren't real. You were pretending they were. I don't know how you did it but I want you to go away." Ben kicked Sam hard on the leg.

Sam fell heavily on to the hard path. Ben kicked him again, in the back this time.

"Don't do that. It hurts." Sam felt like crying. He grabbed his bag and moved away. Ben followed aggressively and Sam felt a shiver of fear run over him.

Suddenly he remembered something. He stopped moving and stood still, facing Ben.

"I will not be afraid of you," he shouted at Ben. "You're a bully, a thief and a liar! You're a pig and I hate you!"

"No need to go that far, mate," came a voice on his right.

Sam knew it was Jake's voice but he dare not turn as Ben had put his bag down and was now getting ready for a real fight.

Sam took a deep breath, "I'm sorry, Ben. I shouldn't have said all that. I was scared and mad at you."

Ben swung his fist and as it connected with Sam's nose blood began pouring out. Sam stood still and Ben again raised his hand to continue the assault. Suddenly he lowered his arm and looked at Sam's nose with blood spilling out over his clothes.

"You look a mess," he said miserably. "I shouldn't have done that."

This was such a change in attitude that Sam knew Jake must have done something to help.

"Sit on the grass and pinch the lower part of your nose." Jake's voice sounded close. Sam did as he suggested and looked up at Ben towering over him. His nose hurt, his leg hurt and he even felt sick.

"I'll be all right in a minute," Sam muttered bravely from behind his hand on his nose. "I shouldn't have said what I did. Sorry again."

Ben stared at him. "You're not mad?"

"I hurt too much to be mad and I think I'm going to be sick." Sam leaned forward.

"You get what you say," came Jake's warning voice. Sam jumped up.

"I'm all right now but I think I'll go home," he told Ben. He picked up his bag and began walking home. The bleeding appeared to have stopped.

"What're you going to tell your mother?" Ben called after him.

"I'll wash out my shirt. She'll never know," Sam answered.

"Well, I'll deny I did it if you say it was me," Ben replied.

"See you, Ben. I won't try and talk to you so please don't kick or hit me again." Sam had reached his gate and, after checking for mail in the letter box, he carried on walking. He hadn't seen Jake but for some reason Sam felt he was nearby.

As soon as he was sure Ben was out of earshot Sam looked around for his invisible friends.

"Where are you?" he called softly. No answer – so Sam walked quickly towards his house, wondering at Ben's frenzied attack and Jake's advice. He needed to hurry so he could wash the blood out of his shirt before his mother saw it.

Now Sam thought about it he felt well again – without pain or anything except the blood to show for what he had been through.

Once he'd washed out his clothes his mother wouldn't know anything had happened. That would be good, he thought, as otherwise she would worry.

She had often told him that Ben wasn't a good sort of friend to hang around with.

She was right, again, he thought. I should have listened to her.

Sam reached the house but paused before opening the door. He could hear the radio in the kitchen which meant his mother was home. He looked down at his shirt. What a mess. Suddenly he remembered the garden hose on the other side of the house and he ducked down low and ran towards it, pulling off his shirt.

The water was cold but the blood washed out. Sam shivered and, squeezing out as much water as he could, he put his shirt back on. Maybe his mother wouldn't notice he was wet, but she sure would notice if he went inside without a shirt on.

He returned to the door and opened it noisily. "Hi, Mum," he shouted as he started towards his bedroom.

"Hello, Sam." His mother appeared from the kitchen. "Did you have a nice day? Oh, is it raining? You're all wet?"

Sam snorted and almost laughed. "No, the hose wet me. I'll go and change. It's cold." He hurried to his room, closed the door and took a deep breath.

Wow, that was close, he thought, glad he hadn't told his mother a lie. He pulled off his wet shirt and grabbed a clean one from his drawer.

"Oh," Sam jumped, surprised to see Jake sitting on the end of his bed.

"Thanks for helping me with Ben. "Did your King send you?"

Jake's face lit up. "I like talking about our King. I'm allowed to take you back to our world if you like and show you around. Would you like to come?"

"What! Now?"

Jake nodded.

"You bet! I'll have to tell my mother though."

"Why don't I meet you in ten minutes at the post box at the end of your road?" Jake jumped off the bed and left the room.

Sam followed Jake outside. "But what if..." he began but stopped as he heard his mother call him.

"Sam! Before you go anywhere else please could you go and mail this letter for me?"

She came towards him with a letter in her hand. Sam gasped. Had Jake known? Had his King told him something before it happened?

He took the letter and looked around for Jake but he had gone again.

"OK, Mum. See you soon," he said. "I won't take my bike this time. I'll walk."

As he expected, the caravan was parked at the side of the road near the post box. Zoe stood outside, waiting.

"Hi Sam. Ready for some sight-seeing?"

Sam laughed. "Yes. Yes. Yes. Is Jake inside?"

11

Jake and Zoe's School

The trip to Jake and Zoe's land seemed too quick for Sam. As before, no sooner had he stepped into the van than Zoe opened another door. He knew they were crossing into a different world and he struggled to understand the meaning of it all. Where was this place?

"We have to pick up some work from school," Jake told him.

"Don't you go there every day."

"No, we only go to collect our work and take it back once we have finished."

"What happens if you don't do it? If you play around or do what you want to do?"

Zoe and Jake stared at each other and then at Sam.

"Look," Jake began. "You need to understand we have our King and we always do what our King wants us to do. It's not like your world."

"Can't you do what you want to do? Not ever?" Sam was incredulous.

"We always do what we want to do," Jake explained. "We love our King and we always want to do what he wants us to do. Come and see our classroom."

"Do you and Zoe have the same classroom? Even though you are older?"

"We only need one room because we're not all there all day. There are different teachers giving out the work and helping us if we are stuck but they all use the same building."

The three children walked down the same road Sam had seen before – past the shops, past a playground and past a huge park. He noticed there was a game of soccer being played.

"Are you allowed to play soccer?" he asked excitedly. "I thought you had to, you know..." He tailed off in confusion.

Jake grinned. "Whatever do you think of us? We like the same things you do. We're not so different are we?"

"Huh! Not so different? You must be kidding."

They reached a large hall-like building and the three of them walked through the gate and up the stony drive. There were several cars parked at the top near the building, all with green lights on the top.

Zoe danced on ahead and ran towards three children who were sitting on a seat outside the hall. She sat down next to them and Jake and Sam continued walking up some steps and through the open, glass doors.

Once inside, Sam gasped. "Hey, this isn't like my school classroom." The tables and chairs had monitors on each table and the wall of the room appeared to be one large screen.

Several of the tables and chairs were occupied and Jake motioned towards an empty one. Sam sat down next to him and watched with interest.

"Hi Jake. Have you finished your geology assignment?" A tall man broke away from a group and pulled up a chair beside them. He nodded at Sam.

"You must be Sam. I'm Greg."

"How do you know my name?" asked Sam in amazement.

Greg laughed, a deep musical laugh. "There are no secrets in the King's country." Turning to Jake he looked expectantly at the monitor in front. "Show me your work."

Jake touched the table and instantly the whole wall in front of them lit up with his work on volcanoes. He explained it all to Greg as he flicked through the pages on the screen. Sam watched with interest.

"That's fine. You've done a good job there, Jake," Greg said. "Now, we need to break it down further and look for the microscopic life associated with these volcanoes. Call me if you are stuck. I'll see you again, Sam." He waved and left them for another table.

Sam looked across at Jake. "Do you have books?" he asked.

"No, it's all done with computers. No paper or books are needed."

"I haven't seen any watches or clocks anywhere. How do you know what time it is?" Sam asked, looking around.

Jake sighed. "Our King needed to bring time into your world," he said sadly. "We don't have a dimension of time here."

Sam stared. "I don't understand. Who is this King?" As he spoke he felt himself falling...falling... and then he felt a warmth all around him and experienced a wonderful, excited and happy feeling.

"This is what I am like, Sam. This is who I am." He felt rather than heard. "I knew you before you were born. I know your mother and father and their mother and father before them. You are going back to your time now, Sam. You'll see Zoe and Jake again on another day."

Sam stayed still with his eyes closed. Eventually, cautiously he opened them. He was in his own room, lying on top of his bed. He heard a tap at the door and his mother put her head round.

"Hello Sam. You've had a long sleep. You must have been tired. Dinner's ready," she added, closing the door.

Sam stretched and stood up. 'The King spoke to me,' he whispered in his head. He stopped and sat back down on the bed. How could he tell his mother what had happened? Yet he felt he must talk to someone or he would burst. How could he say he had been in another dimension in a large white caravan, that he had met some people who could be invisible and that their King could speak to him?

No, he decided. His mother would think he had gone mad.

"Shall I tell Mum?" he whispered out loud. He stood up again and opened the door, brushing the tears away from his eyes. Wow, he thought, remembering Jake say something about there being no secrets in his world.

12

School Playground At Night

"You're very quiet tonight, Sam. Are you all right?" His mother put down her fork and watched her son. He met her eyes and smiled.

"I'm all right," he said. "I've been having some interesting adventures with my friends and I'm thinking about it all."

His mother frowned. "With Ben?"

"I've met a boy called Jake and a girl called Zoe. I met them and their father that time I took Goldie home. They have a caravan and they had parked right by the fish and chip shop." Never tell a lie, he thought.

"How old are they?"

"Jake is about a year or two older than me and Zoe is a bit younger."

"Bring them home one day," suggested his mother. "They could stay for tea. You look different somehow, Sam." His mother stopped eating and stared at her son. "You're sort of glowing."

The ringing phone made them both jump.

"Oh, good, the phone's working again. It's been off for the past few days," she said as she rose to answer it.

Sam jumped up. "I'll get it." He picked up the receiver and recognised Jake's voice immediately.

"Ben and his gang are going to set fire to your classroom at the school tonight."

"Can you stop him?" demanded Sam.

"No, but you can," came the reply. "He's also got some stuff of yours - your bag I think - and he's going to make it look as if you were involved."

"When is he going to do this and what can I do?"

"Go now to the school and speak to them."

"On my own? Should we tell the police?"

Jake's voice began fading as he answered. "Start walking and..." The phone went dead. Sam replaced the receiver and turned to his mother.

"Ben is going to cause trouble. That was Jake on the phone and I need to go and sort it out."

"Not Ben again. Finish your tea and I'll come with you."

Sam sat down and hurriedly finished his food. "I think it's better if I go by myself," he said slowly.

"I don't want you in any fights," his mother answered. "And you're certainly not going alone to the school playground in the evening."

Sam took a deep breath and waited. "I won't be in a fight," he said confidently, grabbing his jacket.

"It's getting dark. I'm going to drive you," insisted his mother.

"How about you drop me off and go to Jane's place and I'll come over and we'll ride back home together? Jane is opposite the school."

"You're not going alone, and that's final. What's happened anyway?"

"Ben has my bag and Jake says he's going to set fire to the school and I'll get the blame."

"Why doesn't Jake or his father call the police?"

"They can't. Nothing's happened yet," Sam felt frustrated.

"All right," she agreed, looking at her son curiously. "What are you going to say to Ben to change his mind? And I'm coming too."

"I don't know yet," Sam grinned, "but something will pop into my mind by the time I see him!"

Although only seven o'clock the clouds were

making the evening appear dark and the few street lights did not seem to make any difference.

"I wish your father was here," murmured his mother, as she parked outside Jane's house.

Sam frowned. He had all this stuff about Ben to deal with and work out and his mother had begun talking about his father.

"You never let me talk about him," he complained. "Now here we are at the school and I have to get out of the car." He turned towards her with his hand still on the door. "Where is Dad?"

"We'll talk later," his mother answered.

"Bet we don't," Sam growled and slammed the car door. As his anger rose to the surface he suddenly remembered Jake's King. He would know. Perhaps Jake could ask him.

Sam left the car and walked across the quiet road. The street lights formed pools of orange light but the night was still very dark.

He wondered where he would find Ben and didn't like the idea of prowling round the dark school looking for him. Who else might be there?

His mother caught up with him. She handed him a whistle.

"Blow this if you need help. I'll stand here and watch out for you."

"How can you help if I'm in trouble?"

Essie Burnside produced a black sport's umbrella from behind her back.

Sam laughed silently and crept towards the school walls. At last he saw a crowd of older boys huddled in a corner near the school library and as he walked towards them, determined not to be scared, he counted at least eight. One of them would be Ben.

Silence fell as Sam approached and then they all started talking at once. The crowd moved, surrounding Sam, making it impossible for him to escape. Now he could tell that Ben was their ringleader.

"Hi Ben," Sam said cheerfully. "What's up?"

"What're you doing here? Who told you to come?" Ben pushed forward and grabbed Sam's coat. The others joined in, pushing Sam backwards and forwards like a ball. His whistle fell out of his pocket and Ben grabbed it.

"What's this for? Huh? Reckon someone's going to help you?"

Suddenly silence fell again, although this time the crowd seemed to be frightened of something. They backed away from Ben and Sam and then with yells of fear took off at high speed towards the road. Only Ben was left.

"Hey, come back. What's the matter?" Ben seemed bewildered as he looked around. "Come back."

Sam couldn't tell what had frightened them. Surely his mother wasn't that scary? Ben didn't seem to know either.

"I bet it was one of your invisible friends," scorned Ben. "If they really exist. Why did you come?"

"I think they're here right now," agreed Sam.

Ben looked from side to side. Now he appeared scared but Sam still couldn't see anybody.

"What were you here for, anyway?" asked Sam.

"None of your business," growled Ben.

"I think you were going to set fire to the school."

"You're nuts. You should leave me alone. You're always hanging around. Go and get yourself your own friends. I don't want to talk to you. Go on, get out of here."

"You were going to set fire to the school," persisted Sam.

"I still am."

He reached out, grabbed Sam's coat and threw

him on the ground. Sam felt his arms being tied together.

"Sam! Where are you? The boys have gone now." Sam could hear his mother calling. Ben didn't seem to notice.

"That will teach you not to keep following me." Ben grunted with the effort and stood back to examine his work. "What are you going to do about that, aye?"

"I'll be fine." Sam's voice sounded muffled with his face in the grass. He twisted round to look up at Ben and was in time to dodge a kick.

Ben had Sam's bag in his hands and with a determined expression on his face came closer to Sam.

"I missed that time but you're going to be covered in bruises tomorrow," he promised.

Sam didn't like to call out to Jake as he thought this would make Ben even more furious. Silently, in his head, he whispered his plea for help. "Help!"

Sam never knew the next sequence of events. He closed his eyes tightly as he felt a rush of air and the next thing he knew he was sitting on the steps of Jane's house with his mother coming up behind.

"Good, you're here. I've been calling."

"Can we go home now?"

"What happened? Did you find Ben? I see you found your bag."

"Yes, Jake helped me sort it all out," answered Sam, wondering what had happened.

"I think it's time to stay away from Ben," his mother said firmly.

"Oh definitely. I won't ring him or go to his place now at all. I only talked to him because I don't have any friends."

Sam sounded miserable. He stood up and they walked to the car.

"Better not to have any friends than have the wrong sort."

"Where's Dad? Why did he leave us? Is he dead?" The questions shot out like little bullets.

"Tomorrow," his mother suggested.

"No, please, Mum. He's been away for nearly six months. I'll put the kettle on for your coffee and then we can talk, tonight."

His mother came into the kitchen after locking the back door and Sam wondered again how Jake had managed to come into his room through a locked door, but then he returned his thoughts to his missing father.

"You know he's not dead, Sam," Essie Burnside said, settling herself at the kitchen table. "He sends us a card every now and then."

"Why did he go away and why won't you talk about it?"

His mother sighed. "He's trying to protect us. We both decided that the less you knew about the problem the better, but now I'm not so sure. Maybe we should go with the witness protection programme and all be together. If we change our names and how we look and move out of this country we can be together. Is that what you want?"

"Did someone go to prison because of him?"

"Several people went to prison and the trouble is they have family who are looking for your father and if they find him they can find us."

"Can I see him?"

"I don't know how to contact him. I truly don't know where he is, Sam."

Sam sat silently thinking over this new development. Zoe and Jake could help, he knew, but he didn't know how or what to ask. Tomorrow he would try and track them down, he decided. They could ask the King for him.

"Thanks for telling me, Mum. I think I'll go to

bed and think again tomorrow about how to find him."

"Don't go asking anyone without checking with me first," she warned sternly.

13

Josh

"Don't forget you've got swimming tonight," Sam's mother called as he hurried through the hall.

"I've got my gear. See you about five o'clock! I'm walking today as it's too wet and windy for my bike."

"Jake, where are you? I need to talk," Sam whispered a few minutes later as he pulled his jacket hood tighter against the wind.

"Hey!" Jake walked beside him, laughing. "You look pretty wet."

"I'm almost at school and I'm a bit late so it's probably a bad time to talk." Sam looked at his watch.

"You called me," Jake pointed out. "What's the problem?"

"Please can you ask your King where my dad is? "And I need some friends. I like invisible ones, but…"

"I know," Jake agreed, hurrying along beside Sam. "I'll talk to my dad about you."

"Not your King?"

"You have no idea how powerful and important the King is," Jake said quietly. "He tells us what to do. I'll see what Dad says about it and I'll find you later."

Sam made his way to his school classroom, hung up his bag and shook the rain off his jacket.

He was surprised to find he no longer had an empty seat next to him. There was a new boy sitting there, sorting out his books.

"Hi, I'm Sam."

"Josh," muttered the other boy without looking at him.

"Have you just moved into the district?"

"Sort of." Josh turned his head away from Sam, and appeared determined to be unfriendly.

The morning seemed to drag with this silent, moody person beside him and Sam was glad when the bell rang for morning tea. The classroom emptied out but Josh didn't move.

"We go outside now because it's stopped raining," Sam told Josh who didn't seem to want to leave his desk. "We're not allowed to eat inside."

"I'll stay here. Haven't got anything to eat anyway."

"Come on," encouraged Sam. "We're not allowed

to stay inside. You can have one of my apples. I've got two."

The boy followed Sam to his bag, took the apple and bit into it hungrily. They wandered out to the netball court and watched some people playing handball.

"Hey, kid, gimme that. Where'd you get that apple?"

An older boy tried to snatch the apple from Josh but he moved sideways, eating quickly.

"I gave it to him." Sam glared at the older boy. "Who are you?"

Josh came back, wiping his hands on his trousers, the apple finished. "He's my brother, Zak."

Zak slapped Josh across the face. "Don't you take anything without giving it to me," he growled and walked away.

"Is he always like that?" Sam asked, looking at the red mark on Josh's face.

"Yep, pretty much," the boy answered.

"What does your dad say? Is he allowed to hit you?"

"My dad… my… haven't got a dad." Josh walked quickly away in the opposite direction. Sam watched him go. I haven't got one either at the moment, he thought.

The week seemed to go slowly with the silent person sitting next to him all day. Sam tried to strike up a conversation several times but the boy refused to talk. As well as that he never seemed to have anything to eat – not even at lunch time.

Once or twice Sam was sure Josh had stolen someone else's food but he didn't say anything. He looked out for Jake and the caravan every day but a whole seven days passed before he saw him.

"How're you getting on with Josh?" Jake met Sam at the school gate.

"How do you know about…? Oh never mind! I don't like him. He doesn't talk, steals food and he's got a horrible older brother. I get the feeling his father might be in prison too."

"Well, you wanted a friend. Why don't you try a little harder to get to know him. Put yourself in his shoes and think what it would be like."

"Oh, come on, Jake. I can't! I want a proper friend. Did you talk to your dad? Jake! Where are you? Jake? Come back!"

Sam thought hard about what Jake had said. What would it be like? He might be lonely but maybe it was better to be lonely than to be hit and bullied all the time with no one to help.

"Can I make a couple of extra sandwiches for Josh, Mum?" he asked the next day at breakfast.

"Of course you can. Doesn't he take any lunch with him?"

"No. And he's got an older brother who hits him all the time too."

"Oh, no," she groaned. "Not another Ben friend!"

Josh was surprised when Sam took out a plastic bag with some sandwiches and an apple and handed them to him.

"For me? Why?"

"I thought you might be hungry. I'll keep an eye out for Zak so he doesn't pinch them. We'll sit back to back so we'll know if he comes. If he does come over, pass them to me and I'll put them in my bag until he's gone. OK?"

From then on Josh was much easier to talk to and he even joined in and played handball with the other kids.

There had been no communication from Jake for five days so on Saturday morning Sam decided to ride around the neighbourhood to see if he could find the caravan. He was almost back home after a fruitless search when he spotted it near the shops. He pedalled faster and stopped outside the open door, wondering if any of the people walking past could see it.

"Hey!" Jake arrived at his side, eating a yummy looking ice cream. "Want one?"

"Yes, please. Where did you get it?"

"We've got them in the caravan. Come and get one." He led the way towards the gleaming white van. Sam followed, glancing from side to side.

"What's the matter?" Jake stopped and frowned.

"Somebody might see me go in," Sam explained.

"No they won't. Come on, follow me. You worry about things too much sometimes."

"Am I invisible to the people here too?" Sam held up his arm and looked at his hand. It looked normal.

"Oh, Sam," Jake groaned. "Don't you know if you behave normally people won't even see you? It's not a case of being invisible. They won't notice you."

"Yes, but can they see the caravan?" Sam asked as they stepped inside. Jake's father, Jon, was sitting at the table reading a printout from the computer.

"Hi boys," he greeted. "You're right on time, Sam. We need your help. I'll tell you while you eat your ice-cream and, yes, Jake did speak to me about your dad and everything is going to work out very soon."

Sam nearly dropped his ice-cream in his excitement. "Hey, that's great! Thank you. Thank you to your King," he added as he saw the hesitation in Jake's eyes.

"It's always 'thank you' to our King. Everything good comes from him."

Jon pointed to a map on the wall.

"We are going to a place called White Island, a small volcanic island off the coast of New Zealand," Jon told them. "This is a private island and people are not supposed to go there without permission. These people have landed and are in trouble as the man's boat key has dropped out of his pocket and they can't get off the volcano."

"Wow, is it a real volcano? Somebody owns it?"

"Yes," Jon answered. "It's owned by the Buttle Family Trust. There are regular tours to the island, even though it is an active volcano. We need you to tell the man where to find his key so they can get away before it gets too dark. All right, Sam?"

14

Landing On A Volcano

Jake opened the caravan door and Sam gasped at the smell of sulphur. They stepped out on to white and yellow rocks and Sam could see steam rising from the rocks around him.

"Watch out where you walk," Jon warned him. "The family you are looking for is out of sight and behind that big rock. The keys are in front of you and down that crack where the steam is coming from. He sat down to tie his shoe laces and they fell out of his pocket. Be careful what you say to them and don't tell any lies. Their launch is moored over there by the sandy beach."

Sam stared around him and down into the deep crack in the rock. The keys and the man's Visa card were clearly visible but he was afraid to put his hand down the steaming hole. Suddenly he laughed out loud. If he had been brought all the way to New Zealand, to this little island to find the keys, then of course he could put his hand into the hole!

"Hey! Where did you come from?" A man and a

woman and two teenage girls came across the rocks to Sam.

"I came with my friends," Sam told them. "Look, I've seen something down this crack."

"Don't put your arm in there," the woman screamed at him. "It's hot! We know because we've been looking for Doug's keys for hours."

Sam grinned at her and reached into the hole. "Is this what you were looking for?" He handed them and the credit card to her. The woman burst into tears and hugged Sam.

"Thank you, oh thank you," she sobbed. "We were so scared we would have to stay here all night until tomorrow when the charter boat comes."

"How did you get here?" one of the girls asked.

"I'm with my friends and I'd better go and find them now."

"We'll come with you and make sure you're all right," Doug said. "After what you did for us it's the least we can do."

Sam thought fast. How could he get rid of these people?

"Wait here and I'll put my head round those rocks to see if they are still there. If I see them, I'll wave to you." Sam scrambled over the rocks before they could answer and then paused to look around. The stench of sulphur made him cough.

"No, no. We can't let you go alone." The man caught Sam up and regarded the landscape. "We'll go together and look for them."

"Jake, Jon, Zoe!" Sam yelled at the top of his voice, looking straight at the caravan which had appeared in front of him. He turned back to the family who had now all climbed up the rocks after him. What could he do? He couldn't step into the caravan. These people would stay on the island to look for him.

"I'll come down to your boat and we'll look from there," he suggested, hoping that once they were all in the boat he could get away.

"That's a good idea. Maybe we can drive around to your boat?"

"I didn't come by boat," Sam told them. "I flew." That wasn't a lie, was it?

"Oh wow, let's go and find the plane," said one of the girls. These people were becoming a nuisance.

They clamoured back down the rocks to the steaming sea where he could see the bobbing speed boat the family had arrived in. They expected him to wade out to it.

"Take off your shoes and hop in," the man told Sam. "We'll drive you around."

"No," Sam told him firmly. "I know where the plane is and if you follow me you will end up here in the dark. Please let's say goodbye now."

"If you're sure…"

"I am. Have a quick trip back. Bye." Sam turned back, and waving at the grateful family he hurried back up through the rocks. Before he went out of sight of the boat he turned and waved. "They're all here. Goodbye!" he yelled and stepped inside the van.

15

Locked In A Garage

Josh and Sam had now become great friends at school. For some reason Josh would not see Sam at any other time but knowing what Zak was like it was probably a good idea.

One day Jake met Sam after swimming and gave him an iphone. "This belongs to Josh. His address is on the back and we need you to go and give it back please."

"I didn't know he even had one," Sam gasped. He looked at the address. "Good. I'll go now. It's just round the corner."

"You need to go home first and tell your mother," Jake told him as he left.

Sam hesitated and checked the address again. He could almost see the house from where he stood. No need to go home first! He wouldn't be long.

Josh's house looked empty with all the windows closed. Long grass grew up close to the brick base and there was a double garage behind the house. He knocked on the door. Nothing. He knocked again, louder and harder. This hurt his knuckles and he was rubbing them when Josh opened it. It wasn't the same Josh from school though. He grabbed Sam and roughly hauled him inside.

"What're you doing snooping around this house?"

"Let go of me, you idiot. I've brought back your phone. Don't worry I'm not staying. I'm on my way home." Zak came into the hall and stared at Sam. He looked at Josh and then at Sam.

"What did you say his name was?" he demanded.

"I'm Sam Burnside. Let me go!" Zak had grabbed him, stopping him from leaving the house.

"You dopey boy, Josh! The man who put Dad in prison is this boy's father. Now he knows where we live and he's given you back that phone I stole for you. The police will be coming soon! I'm going to lock you in the garage and get my two uncles to come and sort you out. We'll teach you for putting our dad in prison."

"Josh! Zak! Don't do this. Let's talk for a minute."

"Na. Talking's over. You're going to get it this time, Burnside."

Zak took off his belt and tied Sam's hands together. He dragged him down the steps and across the path into the dark garage and locked the door. Sam heard Zak call out as he left, "Keep an eye on him, Josh. I'll be about twenty minutes."

"Hey, Josh! Help me get out!" Sam yelled loudly.

"I haven't got a key but I think you could try and get out of the window. My uncles will beat you up and break your arms but if they know I've helped you. They might do the same to me!"

Josh was trying to open the window when Sam heard Zak return. He seemed to be alone and he flung open the garage door.

"Ha, That's what I thought, little brother. You were going to help him escape, weren't you?"

"No. I was …"

"Liar. I'll tie you both up now. The uncles can't get here until about two o'clock tomorrow morning. They've got a job on but I know some other guys who can sort you out."

He punched first Josh and then Sam before wrapping some rope tightly around their arms and legs.

"I'll be back tomorrow morning," he shouted, slamming the door.

"Has he gone?" whispered Sam. "Let's stay quiet for a while in case he comes back again."

"Stupid thing to do to come here, Sam. Now we're really stuck."

"Can you get free, Josh?"

"No." Josh slumped down on the floor and covered his face with his tied-up hands.

"Where do your uncles live? What will they do to us?"

"They live about an hour's drive away. They're Dad's brothers and real mean and they've been trying to find your dad. Why didn't you tell me your father was the detective who made my dad go to prison?"

"Well, you don't talk much about your family. I didn't even know where you lived until Jake gave me your phone to return to you."

"Who's Jake anyway?"

"Don't change the subject," Sam said crossly. "Why couldn't your family leave my father alone? That's why he had to leave us – to keep us safe. Your dad shouldn't be stealing or whatever he did to have to go to prison."

"Dad's been in prison for months." Josh sounded miserable. "We've had to move all over the place as no one pays the rent. Dad used to take Zak and me out at the weekends and while he drank with his mates we would go to the movies or something."

"Where's your Mum?"

"Gone. She couldn't stand Dad and Zak always pinching stuff. She said I could go and live with her but Zak told me he would beat me up every day if I said yes. He got me that phone so I could message her."

"That stolen phone! You're not a very nice family, are you?" Sam sounded scornful.

"Shut up. Who's Jake?"

Sam sighed. How much should he tell this boy? "He comes from a different country and if I ask him he might be able to get us out of this mess."

"Haven't got the phone here, you dummy."

"Jake! Please can you help us get away before Josh's uncles arrive? Jake!" Sam shouted loudly and Josh cringed.

"He would have to climb in the window."

"He might be here now and we can't see him." Sam stared into the darkened garage.

"Well, why wouldn't he say something if he's here, stupid!"

Jake suddenly appeared in a pool of light beside the boys. He looked stern.

"You were told to go home and tell your mother

where you were going. Josh can't see or hear me so don't bother trying to have a conversation. I'll untie you but Josh needs to stay here. We're not going to be able to be friends if you don't do what the King says. Everything I tell you to do comes from him. We only do what the King tells us."

Jake undid the ropes and as suddenly as he had appeared he vanished. Sam stretched and stood up.

"You're free! How did you do that?" Josh reached out his tied hands and stared at Sam when he hesitated.

"I'm going to leave you here," Sam told him sadly. He fumbled over to the window in the dark and pulled it open.

"You can't do that! I'll give you my phone if you untie me!" Sam looked back at Josh who seemed so sad and miserable and desperate. He had to let him free. Surely the King would understand.

Even as he thought this he felt a strong feeling of apprehension. What would happen if he made the King mad? On the other hand Sam knew the King helped people.

"Come on, quick. You can't leave me here!" Josh's voice sounded even more desperate and he began to cry.

"OK." Sam pulled the ropes undone and they quickly climbed through the window and jumped on to the concrete path.

Sam knew instantly he had done wrong and could almost feel the King's anger at his disobedience.

"Quick, let's get into the house and phone the police," Josh said as they ran up the steps.

"What about your brother? Why don't I go home," Sam suggested, standing in the hall.

"Come here for a minute. I want to show you something." Josh opened the bathroom door but without any warning he suddenly pushed Sam inside and locked the door.

16

Sam Disobeys The King

"Got you!" he yelled triumphantly. "You wait till my uncles come now! You're toast."

Sam was stunned, feeling betrayed and angry. He refused to think of Jake and Zoe and Jon, but he remembered the King and trembled. There was so much he didn't understand.

He sat on the bath and thought about everything he knew about the King. He had now made two mistakes and would probably never see the caravan or his invisible friends again. This was far worse than being tied up in the garage. Disobeying the King was much worse than having to face the uncles.

A whisper like a slight wind seemed to murmur inside his head. "Sam, Why didn't you listen?"

"Please help me," Sam said quietly, but out loud. "I promise I'll never ever disobey you again if you get me out of this mess. I mean, I'll never disobey even if you don't get me out of this mess!" He heard a car turn into the drive and braced himself for whatever was to come. The window. Sam stared at the window. How could he open it? Smash it with a towel, now?

With renewed energy Sam grabbed a towel and wrapped it around his hand to stop himself from being cut. He smashed the glass, scrambled up on to the vanity and levered himself head first out of the window.

The path looked a long way below. He half turned and jumped. The car was now parked in front of the garage. Sam dived into the long grass and bushes alongside the drive. Nobody had seen him but he was shaking with fear.

He remembered what seemed like a long time ago when Jake had told him to make sure he didn't fear anything as that was when things went wrong. How can I stop it, he thought? I've disobeyed the King twice and I may never see them all again.

The bushes and long grass concealed Sam but he knew he would soon have to move if he didn't want to be found. He poked his head around a branch and saw two men with Zak. They would have looked menacing in daylight and as Sam watched them from his hiding place he shivered. These people were big strong men. They could easily catch Sam if he decided to run out. He saw them open the garage and listened as Josh tried to explain what had happened. Sam cringed as he heard the men beating Josh and shouting but he knew he couldn't help him by showing himself. If he had listened to the King's advice he would be home by now. However, Josh may still have been beaten.

Sam didn't have his bike as he had come straight from swimming. This reminded him that he didn't have his school bag either. He must have dropped it inside the house, but he wasn't going back for it. He waited until they all disappeared into the house, wondering why they weren't trying to find him in the street.

The door banged; they were coming back out with a powerful torch. Now he knew he had to move!

Sam had never run so fast in his life but with the shouting from behind he kept going. He reached his driveway without tripping over in the dark and realised the shouts from behind had stopped.

Even before he arrived at his gate he was aware of police cars with their flashing lights and he shivered again, wondering if his mother was all right.

"Here he is!" Sam heard a man's voice through his heaving breaths.

"Dad? Is that you? Have you come home?" Sam fell into the arms of his mother and father.

"We've all been looking for you, son." A policeman, wearing a black helmet and carrying a gun squatted down beside him. "Can you tell us where you were and who you were with?"

"I was locked in a garage at…at…" Sam burst into tears. Josh's uncles were going to beat me up. They are chasing me."

"We're going to take Sam home, officer," Sam's father said quietly. "I think he needs to have a hot drink and recover after what he's been through. We can come down to the station tomorrow if that's all right?"

"Of course, Mr Burnside. We'll see you all tomorrow." His radio crackled and he turned away to speak. When he turned back he was smiling. "We've got them. Two men and two boys."

"Please be nice to Josh. He couldn't get away either and he was locked in the garage too," Sam pleaded.

"He'll be fine. We've been trying to take him to his mother for weeks."

17

Sam Has A Surprise

Although Sam was excited about having his father home he felt very unhappy. Would he ever see Jake or Zoe or Jon again?

Would the King ever allow him back to his country? Maybe he would be one of those people who couldn't see the caravan. Maybe it would be an invisible caravan for him too?

The next few days passed in a blur as the government officials met with Sam and his mother and father. They made sure Sam was always with them so there was no way he was able to go and see if the caravan was anywhere.

"We're going to move to a country called New Zealand," Dad told him eventually. "We're going to begin a new life, Sam. You have cousins and I'll have a new job."

"Cousins? I didn't know that. When will we leave?"

"In one week's time."

That week was a busy one for all three of them. They sorted out what they would take with them on the plane and the furniture, books and things which would go into a large container. This would arrive several weeks after they landed so they needed to plan carefully.

Sam had seen nothing of Jake or the caravan. He felt numb and sad inside when he remembered how he had disobeyed the King.

The last day arrived. Sam had said goodbye to his class mates and all was now ready for them to drive to the airport that evening. Josh hadn't been at school as he was now with his mother in a different part of the country.

"Well, here we are, having breakfast on our last day in this country. How do you all feel?" Dad asked, cheerfully. Sad and horrible, thought Sam.

They jumped at the loud knock on the door. "Who's that? We're not expecting anyone." Sam's father opened the door cautiously.

"Come in," Sam and his mother heard him say. "We're having breakfast. Would you like some pancakes too?"

His father led the way into the kitchen with a big

grin on his face. “Sam, a friend has come to see you before we leave.”

“Who…?” Sam began to say. Jake walked in behind his father. He also had a big grin.

“Did you think I’d let you get away without seeing you?” he asked.

“Yes,” Sam answered simply. “We’re going to live in New Zealand so I won’t see you again, will I?” Suddenly he realised that his father and mother could see Jake!

The chatter over breakfast was fun and normal, although Sam could almost feel real pain at the thought of losing contact with this wonderful family of Jake’s. How could he have been so stupid? This must be the last time as it was so unusual for Jake to be visible to people.

“I’ll walk down the drive with you,” Sam said, pushing his chair back when they had all finished.

The moment they were alone, Sam turned to Jake. “How could they see you?”

“Dad wants to talk to you,” he said quietly. “He’s mowing the grass next door.” Now they were alone Jake seemed sombre and serious.

The caravan stood at the end of the drive. Sam

trembled as Jon switched off the mower and came over to speak.

"See you later!" Jake called as he left them.

"I'm so sorry." Sam stood still and looked at Jon. "I disobeyed the King – and He still saved me. Will you ever trust me again?" he ended miserably.

Jon put his hand on Sam's shoulder. "Yes, you will see us again. The King knows you are sorry and that you realise you did the wrong thing. I won't say you made a mistake because you knew exactly what you were doing. Didn't you?"

"Yes, I know and I'm so sorry, Jon. I'll try to always do as you say if I can still see you all sometimes."

"Right, that's settled then. We'll see you in New Zealand. Come and get three ice creams from our freezer and you can take them to your mum and dad!"

Sam's spirits lifted and he now felt the familiar excitement he usually felt when he was with Jon and Jake and Zoe. "Oh, thank you. That's the best news. Now I'm really happy about Dad being home."

The inside of the caravan looked the same although Sam now began to see everything in a different way. The King is real and he's forgiven me!

"Ice-creams! Come and choose your flavours!" Zoe shouted as Sam hesitated on the step.

"Hurry before they melt," Jake advised with a smile. "See you in New Zealand. We'll have lots of adventures."

Sam left them with his hands full and turned for a final wave.

The caravan had disappeared.

18

Visiting The Cousins

The move with his mother and father to New Zealand had been busy and the first few weeks were full of activity for Sam as they decided where to live and where he would be going to school. His parents chose an intermediate school, with both boys and girls in the same classes. He would be there for two years and Sam was in Year 8 – the second year.

At last all the furniture was unpacked and his books on the book shelf, so for the first time in quite a while Sam had begun thinking of his adventures with the invisible caravan and Jake, Zoe and Jon. He sat at his desk, remembering Ben who had tried to make money from selling the clothes Jake had lent them when they went to help the people with the tsunami. Then there was Josh who Sam had believed to be his friend. He decided to be careful who he told about the King and the invisible caravan.

Sam walked into his new school classroom and suddenly knew he would see or hear from his invisible friends. The butterflies were back in his stomach and he could hardly concentrate on what the teachers were saying.

Thinking about the King made his heart beat a little faster. The King had forgiven him, not once but twice and Sam remembered his promise to always obey to do everything the King told him.

"We're planning on visiting your cousins this weekend," Dad had told him on Monday. "Now we're settled we can have a normal family life! We'll drive to Tauranga and stay at Mount Maunganui."

Sam had been waiting for this day to come, when all the police protection plans had been checked out and he could at last meet his cousins.

Today was Friday. When and where would he meet up with Jake? For the first time since he arrived at his new school Sam found the time passing slowly.

"What are you doing this weekend, Sam?" Rebekah asked.

"We're going to Tauranga to see my cousins. Have you been there?"

"Yes. Our team sometimes plays netball with Tauranga Intermediate."

"How far away is it?"

"Oh, it takes us about three hours when we take

the car and about four when we go by bus. See you Monday. Have fun with your cousins."

It wasn't until Sam had nearly reached the library opposite his apartment that he saw Jon walking towards him.

"Jon! Hello! Will I see Jake and Zoe soon?"

"Yes, of course you will," laughed Jon. "Our King has a job for you for tomorrow. Will you help?"

"Yes. Yes. Yes," Sam answered fervently. "I'll do everything right and won't make any mistakes this time."

"Oh, never mind about making mistakes. It's not the mistakes that matter. It's if you deliberately and knowingly go against what you know is right. Do your best, Sam. Jake will talk to you when you arrive at the Mount."

"What will I be doing?"

"We'll tell you at the time," Jon answered. "We work in the present, not the past or the future. Good to see you again!"

Jon ruffled Sam's hair and vanished before his eyes.

"I was going to ask if I could tell my cousins about you," Sam spoke to the empty air. Jon didn't return and Sam hurried home to get ready for the trip.

Saturday morning arrived and with it came high winds and heavy rain.

"Shall we still go?" wondered Sam's parents.

"Yes, let's go, Dad. I've been looking forward to this trip for ever. I'm going to meet my cousins for the very first time."

"You used to see the older ones up to when you were about three," his mother said. "After that they emigrated to New Zealand.

"Who are they exactly? Is my aunt your sister, Mum, or Dad's sister? And how many cousins do I have?"

"Your Uncle Peter is my older brother," his father told him. That makes your Auntie Dot my sister-in-law and also your mother's sister-in-law. They have four children."

"What are their names again?"

"Aaron is nineteen and away at university. Maddy is sixteen and the twins, Chris and Chloe, are eleven, the same age as you."

"Come on, let's go!" Sam danced around the table.

"Bring your swimming gear. There is a hot pool at the Mount."

"This gets better and better."

Sam dashed off to his bedroom and stuffed his swimming clothes into his bag. “Ready Dad? Ready Mum?”

19

Sam Is Devastated

"Dad, look! What's that big bottle over there?"

"That bottle is there because we are in Paeroa, and Lemon and Paeroa, or L&P as it's called, is a famous New Zealand drink. Somebody started bottling mineral spring water about 1915 but now it's all done in a factory. There's another big bottle on the way out of the town too. Who's going to see it first?"

An hour and a half later Sam's family numbered off the Avenues in Tauranga.

"We're here! Eleventh Avenue. There's the house, Dad," Sam shouted excitedly.

"That's what the house looked like on Google Street View. See the brick house with the little white fence, Sam?"

No sooner had the car stopped than they were surrounded by people on both sides. Sam's Aunt Dot opened his door and as his feet touched the ground she hugged him tightly.

"It's so good to see you again, Sam."

At the same time Uncle Peter flung open the passenger door and welcomed Sam's mother. "Hey, Essie, Matt! Good to see you both at long last. Come on in and meet some of my tribe. Maddy is here, and the twins, but Aaron is away at university."

A tall dark-haired boy and similar-looking girl pulled Sam towards them. "I'm Chris, and this is my sister, Chloe. Come with us and we'll show you around."

"Hang on a minute," Uncle Peter said. "Let's all go inside and have some lunch first and then we'll come over to the Mount with you to your accommodation."

"I'm meeting the girls in half an hour so I won't come over, if that's all right, Dad?" Maddie asked.

"That's fine. You can come with us another time," her father agreed.

Lunch was fun and Sam decided he liked these twin cousins very much. If only they lived closer…

They showed him their hut in the garden and told him about some of the adventures they and their friends had after school and in the holidays.

"We sometimes meet them at Pleasure Island, over at the Mount," Chloe said excitedly. "Let's go and see if they are around when we're over there today."

"What's Pleasure Island? Do we need a boat? Does it have a rollercoaster there?" Sam wondered aloud.

The twins fell about laughing. "No, it doesn't need a boat, and there's nothing there like that at all," Chris said at last. "Chloe meant to say Leisure Island. We call it Pleasure Island because we like it so much."

"Why do you like it if there's nothing there?"

"You'll see, you'll see," Chris promised. "Can we go in Sam's car to the Mount, Mum?"

"If it's OK with your Auntie Dot and Uncle Peter. They can follow us but you know the way too."

"Is it all right, Auntie? Do you have room for two more?"

"Heaps of room. Is everybody ready to leave?"

"Make sure you have your jacket and shoes," Uncle Peter shouted after them.

Sam loved being part of a bigger family and enjoyed every moment of the car ride over to Mount Maunganui.

"Is the Mount really a volcano?" he asked, thinking of his trip with Jake to White Island.

"Yes, it is. You can see the steam from another volcano, called White Island, from the top."

"White Island!" Sam stared at Chris. Really? Is that near here?"

"Yep. We've never been over but there are day trips if you and your mum and dad are interested. We turn left into Rita Street in a moment, Uncle."

"That's pretty near both the Mount and the beach," Sam's mother sounded excited. "We'll have to come down here lots of times."

Their beach apartment was small and compact. "It's got everything you need," Auntie Dot agreed. "Kitchen with fridge and microwave, two bedrooms and TV in the lounge."

"Can we go over to our island," Chris asked the adults.

"Island?"

"It's not really an island. It's a volcanic headland which juts out from the beach. Lots of people walk over the tracks every day. Chris and Chloe often meet their friends there and Sam'll be quite safe." Uncle Peter reassured Sam's parents.

"That's all right then. Shall we meet them down there, Dot?"

"Yes, we'll see you on the beach in an hour, Chris. You're in charge," his father told him.

"He's always in charge," moaned Chloe. "I'm the same age too."

"No, you're not. I was born first!"

"Start walking or you can stay here with us," Uncle Peter told them as they left.

"We're not really sure who was born first," Chris explained to Sam. "We're trying to find our birth records so we'll stop arguing about it."

"Can't you ask your parents?" Sam asked.

The twins laughed. "Not really," Chloe answered first. "We're adopted, the same as you are!"

"I'm not adopted. What makes you think that?" Sam stopped and looked at his cousins. "I didn't know you were either."

Chris and Chloe looked at each other and shrugged. "Come on, let's go to Leisure Island and see if Zoe's there." Chloe burst into a fast run.

Sam followed at a slower pace. Did they know a Zoe too? He heard Chris shouting for him to hurry.

The twins were talking to a tall boy who looked a lot like Jake. It was Jake!

"Hi Sam," Jake grinned and then laughed at first Sam's bewilderment and then the cousins'.

"How do you know Jake?" Chris demanded.

"We've been friends for quite a while," Jake said, beginning to walk towards the sea. "Zoe's here too."

"And Jon and the caravan?" asked Sam.

"Who's Jon? What caravan?" Chloe demanded.

"Jon's my dad. We'll show you the caravan another day. Here's Zoe."

"Hi everyone." Zoe jumped up from where she was sitting on the sand, making little piles of shells.

The five children climbed over the rocks to Leisure Island. Sam stayed on the gravel path while the others ducked and dived along different paths in the bushes.

From time to time one of them would run back to try and encourage him to follow them but Sam refused to do anything except follow the gravel path with his head down. Adopted? How could he be adopted? He had always been told his eyes were like his father's?

Eventually they all arrived at the same point and stood on the headland watching the rolling waves.

"Time to go back," Chris yelled and he began running back the way they had come.

Sam plodded along after them. He was no longer excited to be with his family and friends. The day seemed to drag and he had a pool of misery inside. Adopted? Really?

Sam's head was whirring with the information the twins had shared about his being adopted. Was he? He couldn't be. His mother and father would have told him. Wouldn't they? He stared out at the rolling breakers and wondered to himself.

"Earth to Sam. Earth to Sam. The parents are waving to us to come."

Sam continued to dawdle behind the others who were talking excitedly and making some sort of plans. Jake dropped back to speak to him.

"Something wrong?" he asked quietly.

"No, nothing wrong," Sam lied quickly without thinking. "Oh, drat. Sorry Jake, that wasn't true and I'm being careful not to ever lie. The twins are adopted and they've told me I am too. If I am, why didn't Mum ever tell me? I feel betrayed, cheated, weird…"

"Maybe, if it's true, your parents did tell you but you weren't listening?"

"What do you mean, 'not listening'? It's hardly something you'd not hear!"

"There are lots of things the King is probably telling you but you may not be hearing."

"Does your King really talk to me? Why wouldn't I hear him? Anyway, surely I'm not adopted?"

"Would it be so bad if you were?"

"Yes!" Sam answered firmly.

"What has having the same blood got to do with it? Your Mum and Dad aren't related. Zoe and I have to go now but we'll see you another day."

"Jon said something about he needed me to do something here in Tauranga?"

"Yes, but now we think you've got plenty to do and sort out, don't you? See you, Sam. Bye guys."

Sam turned back to the twins and walked silently beside them to the four adults sitting on the beach.

"You OK, Sam? You've gone very quiet. Is this about the adoption thing? We really thought you knew."

Sam longed to shout, "Shut up, shut up" at Chris. "Don't talk to me" but he just shrugged and muttered that it was all right, which of course it wasn't at all.

20

Sam Meets The King

Sam waited until they had arrived back home in Auckland before speaking to his parents about his adoption. Essie and Matt wondered why he had been so quiet since his excited arrival in Tauranga. They couldn't decide what had happened to their happy son but thought it better to let him tell them.

"If he hasn't said anything by tonight I think we should ask him what's wrong," Essie suggested to her husband.

"Ask who what's wrong?" Sam had been so quiet his parents hadn't noticed he was in the same room.

"You! You've been so quiet and unhappy since we went to Tauranga and we thought you got on well with your cousins?"

Sam looked from one parent to the other. Now was the time. Was he brave enough to hear? He took a deep breath.

"Am I adopted?"

"Yes, of course you are. We've always told you that," his parents looked bewildered.

"You have not," Sam shouted, throwing his book on the floor. "I didn't know until the twins told me. How could you not tell me? Where did I come from? Who am I?"

Matt reached over to his son but Sam pushed him away, almost sobbing now.

"You didn't tell me. How can you say you did?"

"Listen son…"

"I'm not your son!" Sam stamped his foot. "Who am I?"

"Sam!" The whisper sounded loud in his head. *"You're hurting them by speaking like that."*

His mother wiped away her tears and reached out to hug him. This time Sam stayed still, and stiff.

"Sam!" Another warning from the King.

The King had really spoken to him! Suddenly Sam's adoption issue took second place. The King had spoken to him! He turned to his father who looked so sad and then to his mother.

"I'm sorry. I shouldn't have said that and I don't really mean it. I had such an awful shock when the twins told me I was adopted and I felt so mad you didn't tell me. When did you tell me?"

"We've always told you that you were special and that we chose you."

"I didn't know that meant you adopted me. I thought you wanted me."

Essie laughed through her tears. "We did and we do want you."

In the days following, Sam and his parents thought he had finished with being sad about his adoption. However, Sam began to feel hurt and upset all over again.

He stayed in his room, listening to music or trying to read a book and hardly spoke to anyone at school. He kept going to swimming and his music lessons but he was getting more and more depressed.

"You're going the wrong way. Turn back." Sam ignored the warning in his head but he didn't understand it anyway. Turn back from what?

Who were his real parents and why did they give him away? He didn't want to talk to Essie and Matt about it anymore and there was nothing they could say to him to make him feel better. The whole family were under a black miserable cloud.

Sam hadn't seen the caravan anywhere and was so unhappy he didn't even bike around to look for it.

"Wrong way. Turn back." There it was again. What did it mean?

"Sam!" Jake caught him up as he walked home from swimming. "Come with me and see Zoe and Jon for a few minutes. We want to ask you to help a family who are trapped in a cave and the tide is coming in fast."

"Sorry," Sam muttered, breaking into a run. "I'm in a hurry to get home. Find someone else."

"Wrong way. Turn back."

"Sam!" Jake stood still and yelled after him. "We need you."

Sam carried on to his house and hurried into his room, slamming the door.

"Sam," his mother tapped on the door. "Is everything all right?"

"Yes," he lied. "I'll be out for dinner in a minute."

"Sam, that was a lie." Sam knew this was the King speaking but he turned his mind away – not letting the warm love from the King surround him.

The next day Sam felt even worse. He didn't

actually hurt anywhere but he almost felt ill with being so miserable.

He didn't go to school but kept walking until he came to a park with trees and swings and seats. He sat on one of the seats and stared at the trees. He couldn't even be bothered thinking of anything.

Slowly, ever so slowly, Sam sensed warmth in the air.

"Sam, what are you doing here?" The warmth wasn't from the sun.

He jumped as he saw a man sitting on the park seat next to him. Sam had never seen the man before and they stared at each other. There was a warm light surrounding the man. He was glowing, as Jake had been once.

"Sam," said the man again, very quietly. "What are you doing here?"

Sam tried to stand up but his legs had turned too wobbly for him to move. Surely this was the King? He kept staring at the man.

"Who are you?" he whispered, turning hot and cold.

"You know who I am. You hear my voice."

"But Jake said he never sees you. You are a man."

"I'm looking like a man because I need to speak to you. Come with me," he commanded, reaching out his hand.

At the touch of the man's hand Sam could have fainted with the love, joy and peace which flooded him. He closed his eyes and sighed. When he opened them he saw they were standing on a mountain with mountains and hills all around. Some had snow on the top and there was a winding river in the valley. He could hear birds singing and everywhere was still and beautiful.

"You have trapped yourself into a little, dark room, Sam. Each time I told you to turn back and that you were going the wrong way you slammed another door against me. You decided not to talk to anyone. You wouldn't get any help from Jon and Jake and Zoe. You lied to your mother. You also refused to help that family Jake told you about. Those were my instructions you disobeyed. Each time you were shutting me out. You knew what you were doing but after a while it became too hard to get out of your little, dark room. I'm here to help you."

"I'm adopted and I want to know who my real parents are and why they gave me away. I haven't got any friends."

"Stop feeling sorry for yourself, Sam." The King's

voice was gentle but firm. "Remember the boy at the swimming squad who asked you what you did to swim faster than him? He wanted to be a friend. What about Rebekah who asked you if you were going to the school disco tonight? She wants to be friends. Then of course there's Jon, Jake and Zoe. You will find your birth parents in the future, but not yet. Those questions will be answered but now is not the time and you need to accept this. I also think it's about time you told your parents you know me. You haven't realised it but they also hear my voice."

Sam gasped. "They know you? I can tell them everything?"

"Don't you remember Jake telling you that there are no secrets in our land?"

Sam took a deep breath. "Will you help me get back to normal? Please? I'm so sorry I messed up. Again."

The King took Sam's hand again. "Come and see Jake. He's sitting in his classroom looking at volcanoes and thinking of you!"

Sam saw he was outside Jake's school. The day was beautiful and he felt wonderful.

The King was no longer with him but Sam felt

well. He had escaped from his little, dark room and he decided that he would never again keep taking those steps which led him into it.

He walked up the path and into Jake's classroom. Jake didn't see him and Sam sat down next to him.

"Sam!" Jake gasped. "How did you…You've been with the King! Wow! Sam! Did he bring you here?"

Sam laughed. "Yes, he brought me to see you. He said you were looking at volcanoes and thinking of me. How did you know I had been with the King?"

"You're glowing all over." Jake saved his work and stood up. "Let's go to my house. I'll show you what I've been doing lately."

www.ingramcontent.com/pod-product-compliance
Ingram Content Group UK Ltd.
Pitfield, Milton Keynes, MK11 3LW, UK
UKHW020128250726
13967UKWH00002B/541

9 780995 111783